"My favorite reading exp  by story and exhilarate nique. That's what this (stories are distinctive, powerfully moving, and exquisitely well-written. Please join me in the Bess Winter Fan Club."

—Chris Bachelder, author of *The Throwback Special* and 2016 National Book Award Finalist

"No one writes quite like Bess Winter. Her stories are at once playful and mournful, so witty and so clever, and yet also haunted by the specter of lost things and lost time. *Machines of Another Era* draws readers into the lives of creators and collectors, of anachronistic characters tinged always with the yearning of nostalgia as they care for garnets and dolls and even postagestamped babies. These stories are sharp and lush and an absolute pleasure to read."

—Anne Valente, author of *The Desert Sky Before Us*

"It's customary, I suppose, to say something like 'Bess Winter is a writer to watch,' but she's not: Bess Winter is a writer to be utterly transfixed by, a writer to gape and goggle at. The varied and splendid stories in *Machines of Another Era* are marvels of compression, of invention, and of lyricism."

—Michael Griffith, author of *Trophy*

"I loved these stories, each as precisely cut and shimmery as a jewel. Bess Winter conjures moments out of history with a virtuosic combination of research and imagination. In her hands every object is a magical one, every life a fantastic tale."

—Leah Stewart, author of *What You Don't Know About Charlie Outlaw*

MACHINES OF ANOTHER ERA

MACHINES OF ANOTHER ERA

BESS WINTER

GOLD WAKE

CONTENTS

For
Vida,
Breffni,
and Wendell

MACHINES OF ANOTHER ERA

SIGNS

It is after a series of nubile young researchers have begun to parade through Koko the gorilla's life that she learns the sign for *nipple*. She draws her heavy arms close to her chest, and her leathery pointers spring out towards the unsuspecting graduate student. A look of expectation settles onto her simian face. Sometimes her gaze rests on the soft sloping clavicle that betrays itself from beneath an unbuttoned collar, sometimes on the ponytail that rests coyly on one shoulder like a thick tassel, and sometimes on the face of Dr. Thomas, senior supervising researcher, as if she's asking him whether she's doing it right.

Inevitably, the student looks to Dr. Thomas. *What should I do? What should I say?*

Nipple, signs Koko.

Inevitably, Dr. Thomas tells her it is her duty, as a paid researcher, not to interfere: that she should indulge Koko's fetish, that this, too, should be researched.

Inevitably, there is a long moment while the student struggles with the request. Dr. Thomas fumbles his pencil, tapping it against his notepad, twirling it between two fingers. He does

1

this until the student takes in a long reedy breath, looks down to unbutton her blouse with shaking hands.

Then there is the moment where she peels off her blouse and unhooks her bra, and the moment where she sets the bra beside her on the table or hangs it by one strap over the edge of the chair.

Dr. Thomas knows there are two types of graduate students: the ones who put their bras in front of them on the table and the ones who hang them behind themselves on the chair. They may be further categorized by type of bra: underwire, sports. Then there are those who don't wear bras at all. He can never predict which students will not be wearing bras, except that these young women are usually small-breasted, gamine.

And there is the inscrutable moment between woman and beast where the researcher, breathing fast, sits half-clad in front of the gorilla, and the gorilla does not sign at all. Where the researcher, avoiding a direct gaze into the gorilla's eyes lest she provoke her, cannot avoid Koko's gaze because Koko seems to address her directly and without words. Dr. Thomas jots down notes, but he cannot understand why, in this moment, Koko reaches out to take the students' hands. He can only hypothesize about why some graduate students cry at the slightest touch and why some smile at the gorilla, why some curl into Koko's arms when she opens them. Why some allow her to touch and gentle them, to trace their eyes and nose and soft neck with her rough fingers. Why some nod knowingly, and why the gorilla nods back, and why he feels a sudden shift in the room, as if he's the unwelcome guest at a sacred rite.

He can only guess at this, too: why, after each student leaves for the day and it's just Dr. Thomas and Koko, the gorilla regards him with a withering look. Why she pokes at her fruit and then looks up at him like a wife waiting to broach a touchy topic at dinner.

And why, when she finally signs to him, *nipple,* he searches her earth-brown eyes for some silent instruction. If there are words in those eyes, he can't find them. Those eyes are deep and ripe. They're unmapped territory. He doesn't know whether to remove his shirt or call back a graduate student. With a shy hand, he touches his collar and makes to open it. But before he completes the gesture the moment passes, or he has done the wrong thing already. Koko looks away.

A BEAUTIFUL SONG,
VERY MELANCHOLY AND
VERY OLD

That summer, flies sang around the trash heaps and grocery stands and alleyways of Toronto. Millions of flies, humming and darting about the head, landing on collars and cheekbones and lips, rubbing polluted legs together before lighting off for road apples fresh-plopped from some wormy cart horse, then onto swinging meat at the St. Lawrence Market, the nipple of a baby's bottle, or a roll of sanitized gauze at the Victoria Hospital for Sick Children, waiting for an open wound.

The flies were luck for Leland, who came home from the leather factory dyed completely red, pinching a clipping from the *Star*. The clipping had been passed among the men who worked in the dye yard, so it was colored at the edges: oxblood and blue and bruise-yellow. But Leland had snuck away with it, and he'd held it, careful, scared he might fold it into a red pocket or clutch it in a red hand.

Again, his teenaged daughter Myrtle waited at the doorstep. Her disappointed look already fixed, like she'd worn it all day in anticipation of his return. She braced herself against the jamb, pinning the screen door wide open while the flies wheeled in and out of the house. Even her hair ribbons seemed to wilt in the heat of July. A fly settled on a loose ribbon's end. Myrtle slapped it away.

She eyed the clipping Leland held up like some flimsy standard. *What's that?* she asked.

Music lessons. Leland gave a flourish in imitation of a conductor and tucked the clipping into the pocket on Myrtle's apron.

Myrtle retrieved it, read it aloud.

GRAND PRIZE COMPETITION

SWAT THE FLY!

MILLIONS OF FLIES ARE TO BE ASSASSINATED

The Fly Has Got No Friends, and He Does Not Deserve Any—He Carries Disease to the Baby and Fills the City Cemeteries.

The newspaper would award a youth, aged sixteen or younger, fifty dollars—a fortune, for a youth—for killing the most flies. Carcasses would be received at the Health Office on Tuesdays, Thursdays, and Saturdays between four and five p.m. Breeding of flies strictly prohibited. Fly breeding was a public nuisance and a menace to health. The object was to make Toronto a flyless city, to obliterate the unstopping buzz and the teeming maggot patch.

You're just the one to win it, said Leland.

I don't know how to slap but a couple flies. Myrtle worked her heel against her ankle, after some itch.

To catch thousands of flies, a girl needs a trap.

I don't know about traps.

Don't you know I'll make you the traps, stupid? How many times have I gone fishing with a whole coffee can full of flies? We've got enough flies right here in Cabbagetown to fill barrels! He motioned past the skimpy yard. There on the street, as if he'd called her up, the Rag Lady passed with her reeking cart, her gray hair knotted into terrible burrs.

How many music lessons does fifty dollars buy? asked Leland. *You'll have enough music lessons to take you to Carnegie Hall.*

Mother says supper's ready, said Myrtle. She turned back into the house, letting the screen door slap closed before Leland could follow.

Only mistrust from the girl, who scowled at Leland over the dinner table, the steaming crock of purple cabbage and the boiled corned beef. Flies settled on the food. A crazy waving of hands to shoo them, the whole family waving: Leland, Minnie, and their six daughters, all crushed around the meal. Myrtle's face, crimped and sour as the cabbage. Leland could hardly watch her without feeling soured, but he still cared for Myrtle. Why? Why this bitter one, this lanky, homely one, fifteen-and-a-half, who now spat the fatty end of her meat, well-sucked, back onto her plate? Again, she looked at him and her look was daggery, but she was the only one who ever looked. Hardly even a hello from Minnie and the other girls, who'd given up on Leland and let him buzz past and around them, in and out of the house at any hour, reeking of skins and dye and whatever else he'd soaked up. Sometimes he brought home all his pay. Often, he didn't. He could find a million ways to lose it, to drink it, to disappear it on a bad bet. Only Myrtle even mustered the energy to be disappointed, now. Only Myrtle would ask him for a thing like music lessons.

After supper, Myrtle gave her weekly recital. The whole family, sisters and mother and father, squeezed into the space of their parlor, settled onto each other's laps so they could fit in that small room with its thick wallpaper and its modest portrait of the King. Flies knocked the globe of the coal-oil lamp, keeping strange time as Myrtle worked the concertina. It was as if she was transported, her lashes fluttering when she reached for the high notes, her look peaceful as those of the plaster Virgin Marys in the yards Leland passed on his walks to the dye yard. Each Mary possessed of her own strange beauty, sheltered by a grotto made from leftover bricks or a half-buried bathtub.

After Minnie and the girls were asleep, Leland went for his old flytrap. It had been in the shed for years, the nails that held it together rusted and gritty from age, but its mesh was still solid, and it stood upright when he placed it by Myrtle's bedside, scooted a plate of Myrtle's chewed fat and other supper scrapings underneath its funnel. Drumroll of flies against the windowpane, yearning for the gaslight out on the street. Myrtle, crowded into the bed with two other siblings, flopped in her sleep, mouth open, arm slung across her sister. Leland wanted to reach out, brush back the hair that lay across that moony face. Before he could, a fly landed on Myrtle's eyebrow. He watched it rest there, legs rubbing, before it caught the scent of the scraps and landed underneath the flytrap's funnel. Leland backed away, careful not to make a sound.

Next morning, like all mornings, Leland left for the dye yard before the sun had even crowned on the horizon. He would work the ochre pit, so he wore the trousers and shirt he wore on ochre days, dyed not the lush deep ochre of the skins he sloshed around the pit but a cheap yellow that fellows at work said was because of his bargain clothes, their skimpy fiber that drank the dye.

Fellows at work talked of flies. Everyone had a kid, or twelve kids, and the kids were all out swatting, trapping, drowning flies.

Spyros, who was Greek, had two little girls who'd hung so much flypaper he'd got his face stuck when he'd risen in the middle of the night to take a piss. One fellow, a black man come west from Halifax called Henry, said his little boy put a pin through each fly and stuck them all on the sides of Twenty Mule Team Borax boxes so he could keep count. And Jim O'Brien, that braggart from Sackville Street, red-faced and brown-toothed and too-smiling, just said his kids would win.

All nine of 'em working together. Working all the time, working harder than you or me.

He said this, then left the knot of men looking after him as he trotted back to the blue pit, still wearing his stupid smile.

Wouldn't you like to knock that caca-eating grin right off his face? asked Spyros.

I'd pay to take a swing at him, said Henry.

Leland stared after O'Brien, who eased himself into the chilly blue pit, lifting his heavy arms like in prayer.

That night, Leland stopped at the pub. By the time he got home, supper was over, and kids were playing outside. A pleasant feeling, he thought, walking down a purpled summer street where kids played stick-and-hoop. Today, they all seemed to be at the same game. Everyone had a promotional fly swatter, courtesy of the *Star*. They swatted any fly that landed, on a lamppost or a fence or the back of a hand. A girl commanded her little brother to stand still while she swatted the top of his head. Many cupped their spoils in their palms or tumbled them, loose, into pockets.

Myrtle waited on the stoop. She watched the street's action with detached amusement. Beside her, the busy flytrap. *I've emptied it eight times already.*

Beneath the trap, a plate of rotting chicken livers, scrounged from who-knows-where, rainbowed in the heat.

They like liver most of all, she said.

Leland staggered back a step. *Good girl.*

Tomorrow's Saturday, she said. *First counting day.*

You'll have all the flies by then.

Don't joke about it. You'd better get something to eat, or I'm gonna use the leftovers.

Counting day. Myrtle was a long time in the Health Office. She'd gone in with a big box of flies she'd lugged up the stairs, refusing Leland's help. Leland sat on the steps of City Hall, watching kids arrive with their fly loads. Jars, cans, biscuit tins, buckets, baskets, handkerchiefs; some even had upturned hats full of flies, which they watched with concentration as they climbed the big stone staircase. Some were bothered by living flies as they went. More than one jar shattered before its contents could be counted, on account of a kid waving off a fly. And a whole gang of kids seemed to come and go from the slum next to City Hall. The slanty houses, the curious smoke that rose in places, the piles of dismembered furniture.

Queen Street hummed with its usual action: carriages and bicycles and cars. A streetcar ground to a stop, letting off another load of rushing flycatchers. A policeman on horseback halted in front of Leland.

Everything alright, sir? Think it's time to move along?

My girl would like to trap those, said Leland. He pointed to where the horse lashed at its haunches.

Oh, a fly hunter, eh?

She wants music lessons. You should hear her sing.

And here was Myrtle, up beside Leland, holding her empty box. She smiled.

How'd it go in there? asked the policeman.

They put my name on the leader board.

Very good! Is this man your father?

Sure he is, she said.

Well, said the policeman, who looked at Leland a touch too long, *good luck.* He and his horse lumbered off to where two little flycatchers bit and kicked each other while kids cheered and stomped the pavement.

Are you number one? asked Leland.

So far, said Myrtle. *But it's not even five, yet. And look at her.*

A little girl, no more than seven and dressed in a filthy pinafore, climbed the stairs to City Hall. Her demeanor that of a princess: chin raised, calm downcast eyes. She held a promotional fly swatter as if it was a scepter. Behind her, three young men—her brothers?—hoisted an old whisky barrel. Its bung knocked crooked into the hole by a hammer or a fist.

Looks like it's from the Wheat Sheaf, said Leland.

How many flies can that hold?

Well, that barrel holds enough rounds to make a hundred men happy. So, I'd say maybe three million flies.

You've gotta make more traps, then.

The backyard was bald, and long, and good for trap-making. Leland sent Myrtle to the Rag Lady to get some stockinet or mesh to cover the frames he fashioned from old table legs and pieces of trellis and kindling and other scrap wood. She came back with a clutch of soiled tea dresses and the kitchen scissors, and cut the mesh away from the linings while Leland sawed and hammered. He remembered wanting, as a young man, to build things with his future son. Things like soapbox racers and birdhouses. But, somewhere, he'd forgotten he'd ever wanted to build things in the first place. Minnie had given him no sons.

Myrtle careful-stretched the mesh over the frames, hammered it in place with finishing nails. She worked quick with a hammer. Leland had never seen her use one before, but he supposed Minnie had put her to work around the house. She was capable.

Leland. Here was Spyros, come through the back gate. *We're going out.*

A hand waved from out in the alley, beyond the fence.

Is that Henry?

That's him, said Spyros. *Come on, we're leaving.* He looked around. *Making something?*

Fly traps, said Myrtle, defensive. *We're very busy. We have to make at least ten more.*

Fly traps? This directed at Leland. *My girls gave that up already. Looks like your girl's in it to win, though.*

She is. Leland smiled over at Myrtle. She crossed her arms, wore a hurt expression that might send a zip of shame through any father's heart.

We planned on putting some traps back here today, and some out in the alley and the lot next door, she said.

Flies don't stand a chance, said Spyros.

Here was a moment Leland would look back on, eventually, when he let himself look back. The small moment—and that worse moment, later—when he thought he maybe should stay with the girl.

Instead he said, *Getting dark. We'll finish the rest tomorrow. Rag Lady give you any change?*

Myrtle sighed, dropped the quarter into his outstretched palm. *She wouldn't take my money. Told me to pay her when I win.*

The shining quarter sat heavy in his palm, heads up. His Majesty seemed to snub him, looking off into the distance at something, or someone, far more important. A snatching feeling came over Leland that the Rag Lady, that strange sorceress, had cast a spell on the quarter. That he shouldn't spend it, that no change should ever be made of it, and that it should always travel with him in some pocket.

So, he didn't spend it at the pub, but used other loose change instead. Word was going around of a little girl, no more than seven, who lived just two doors down from the biggest manure heap in the city. It stretched two hundred yards along Fort York, where brave redcoats had once fought invading Americans. Fellows said the little girl could kill scores of flies just by standing by that heap and clapping her hands. Leland thought of the little girl he'd seen with the whisky barrel, and the strong young men who bore that barrel: strong enough to fight off Americans, themselves.

Jim O'Brien was in the pub. He reeled on his barstool and brayed and said there's no way some little girl was going to beat all nine of his kids. Just look at the numbers; it was impossible. He swaggered and came up behind Leland and Spyros and slung his arms around them, swatting Henry on the shoulder with a free hand. His breath on their cheeks, beer and pickled eggs.

Your little ones still chasing flies?

Leland's is, said Spyros.

She's a champ, said Henry. *You don't even know.*

That right? O'Brien looked at Leland, who only clenched his jaw. Then he turned to Henry. *You even allowed in here?*

Like a sudden spooked horse, Henry stood, glared, gripped Jim O'Brien's collar, loosing a fly that had been resting there. O'Brien's eyes, mean little pits. Leland and Spyros stood too, and suddenly every fellow in the bar stood and their voices were up, each man hooting for one fellow or the other, and then all four of them were on the stoop, pushed by the bartender who hollered at them to get out, just get out, you louts.

O'Brien stalked off, cursing, but the thought of him lingered. Leland and Spyros and Henry, wordless conspirators, went straight away back to Leland's house, to where Leland's tools waited, strewn around the backyard and covered in dew. They lit some old lanterns and began to saw wood, hammer together more traps. Light bloomed in the high windows that looked down on the yard. Here was Minnie, hair done in rags, yelling at the men to sober up, to get on home, they'd lose a finger or worse messing with that saw in the dark.

But, by Sunday, Myrtle had fifteen traps. Leland woke to the peal of church bells. A headache buzzed behind his eyes. Myrtle was out in the yard with a big stick, stirring up the flies that settled under the funnels. Flies zipped up and into the traps, sizzled against the mesh, waiting to be doused with bug powder. Myrtle looked up from her work and saw Leland in the window. She waved.

∽

While the men worked, flies swarmed around the dye pits, expired in the heat, pocked the surface of the water. Leland could swing a hand around and skim a thousand flies off the green pit, the blue pit, the red pit. Ochre showed the most flies.

Fellows at the leather factory talked about Myrtle. She was at the top of the leaderboard at the Health Office, followed close behind by Effie B, who must have been the little girl with the manure heap and the barrel and the brothers. In third place, O'Brien. No one let him alone about it.

All nine of your kids can't keep up with two little girls, eh? Spyros called from where he was up to his waist in blue dye. O'Brien sloshed around, sopping and red.

You think you seen flies? He yelled. *You ain't seen nothing yet. They're just getting started, okay?*

Leland was a hero at the pub. Fellows he hardly knew bought him drinks when they saw him. They all raised their glasses to Myrtle, and Leland felt a wash of pride.

And maybe Myrtle felt a little more pride in him, too. Something in her look. The next two counting days, after work, he met her coming out from the Health Office. The girl smiled. A big knock-toothed smile that could only belong to a champion. Little kids buzzed around her—*hey Myrtle, hey Myrtle*—and it felt fine to hear her tell them to get lost. Even the policeman they'd met, Officer Ernie was his name, tipped his hat to Leland and Myrtle when she came out with her empty crate.

How'd you do?

I'm number one!

Officer Ernie stopped, looked Leland up and down. The horse seemed to look at him too. *You're all green, Sir.*

And Leland pointed to himself with pride. *I'm a dye man,* he said.

Walks home after counting: the best walks. Sometimes Leland had enough change for the two of them to take the streetcar to Parliament Street, where they could watch the action rushing by on the sidewalks. But it was better to walk home together all the way from City Hall, through the bustle of those sidewalks, seeing each person right up close. Here was an old man, wrinkled and browned as a dried apple and muttering in Polish, clutching two live rabbits that peeked back at onlookers with wide and world-frightened eyes. Here a Chinese grandmother in housedress and slippers argued with a Kosher butcher over a chicken. Here two Armenian brothers, twins, zigged past on a motorbike with a wicker basket seat, one driving while the other cradled a wooden camera case. And here were heaps of refuse, slumped against buildings and hurled into the street, swirling with flies and choking the air with their stench. Myrtle and Leland took everything in, the Rag Lady's quarter jangling in Leland's pocket the whole time.

These walks allowed miraculous conversations. Conversations like what Leland imagined might happen between fellows in advertisements in *Life* magazine and their apple-cheeked children. Myrtle had dreams. She pronounced them. She thought she might be a fine nurse. She was very good at taking care of other people, especially her sisters, whom she'd had a hand in raising, didn't he think? Or, maybe she could teach piano once she'd learned it herself. But she'd have to have a piano for that.

What did you want to be when you were young?

Leland stopped, looked up at a fat pigeon that hopped along a telephone cable, as if the bird might call back the memory.

I suppose I didn't want to be anything.

Myrtle frowned.

I suppose, continued Leland, *I might have wanted a wife and a family.*

Myrtle hitched the empty box up higher under her arm and stood smiling at him, a real smile, no sarcasm. The smile of her little girlhood. He remembered this smile.

Another memory: the first time he held her. The midwife had told him to be careful; this was a baby, not a sack of flour. So, he was careful. Scared, even. This body, very light, and this glistening gummy open mouth. A warmth he couldn't identify, that seemed to push up from some deep part in him, and the thought: I will do my best. The next thought, an ugly fear that straggled up: my best has never been any good.

The leaders in the Swat the Fly Competition would be photographed for an article in the *Star*. When Leland got home after work that Friday, Myrtle was gone to the *Star* offices, and the stuff under the traps was teeming. Myrtle's stick, a piece of busted trellis still poky with nails, rested up against the side of the house. Leland took it and stirred the maggoty gizzards underneath the traps, sending whole families of flies up the funnels.

This was when the newspaperman came upon him for an interview. He was sure glad, he told Spyros and Henry the next night at the pub, the fellow had found him in action, stirring up those traps.

They held the article, passing it between them. Here was the group photo: the top twenty flycatchers, all lined up in two rows. Myrtle was the oldest and tallest, by at least a head. She wore her white Sunday dress. The O'Brien kids stood all together. They had the same face. O'Brien's face. That stupid smirk.

There were more kids too, some so filthy they must have been those he'd seen coming out of the slums in the Ward. The little girl with the barrel was there beside them, chin raised.

And here was Leland, described right in the first paragraph. *This doting papa, who guards his daughter's traps to ensure maximum extermination, says his Myrtle, the current frontrunner, deserves the top prize when the final count is made this coming Tuesday.*

A tap on Leland's shoulder. A leather factory fellow he hardly knew, a young one who buzzed around O'Brien. He wore the put-upon look of a hard-drinking man saddled with a new family.

Listen, he said. Voice almost too low to be heard. He glanced around. *I been hearing things about your girl.*

Leland turned around, leaned his elbows back on the bar. *Things?*

Some guys, they know where you live. They're saying they're going to bust her traps.

In the far corner, O'Brien and his pals hooted over an arm-wrestling match. O'Brien was referee. He stood with arm raised, like to show he was most important. He was always surrounded by young fellows, still too new-hatched to know what was good.

Who said this?

Just some guys.

Well, when are they going to do it?

The fellow shrugged. *That's all I know.*

Henry leaned right into the fellow's face. *You know more than that.*

I don't, even.

Why you telling me this? asked Leland.

I don't know. Guess I think it's not right.

You know anything at all? asked Spyros.

The fellow shrugged again, shrugged as he backed off for the door.

Tom! O'Brien called to him. He slapped the victor of the arm-wrestling match on the back. *Ain't you going to beat this ruffian?*

But Tom was already gone.

Sunday, Leland and Spyros and Henry hung around the yard, waiting for O'Brien. Myrtle stayed out there too, bothering the stuff under the traps with her stick. It was maybe the hottest day of July. Sun gnawed on shoulders and tops of heads. A little boy, two or three years old, came naked into the yard and sucked his thumb, smiling while his mother called after him. When the men laughed and raised their bottles to him, he toddled away.

The four sat in the shade. Myrtle had her concertina, and she played it with her eyes closed. A beautiful song, very melancholy and very old. Leland closed his eyes, too. As soon as he did, she stopped.

Is it unseemly? she asked.

Is what unseemly?

A young lady of fifteen like me being out here alone with you fellows?

Nothing wrong with it. Keep playing.

The day unwound. Dusk pinked the edges of the sky. Myrtle went back in the house, and soon there were voices and the sound of clinking silverware and pots and pans. Stars came. Myrtle brought out plates of pork and beans and they sat with their suppers. And some hours after that, she said she couldn't keep her eyes open a minute longer. Spyros and Henry said they'd better get home.

What about O'Brien? asked Leland.

He ain't coming tonight, said Spyros. He staggered to the back gate.

That means he's coming tomorrow.

We'll be here tomorrow, said Henry. *We! Will! Be! Here!*

But they weren't. Next day, soon as work was out, Spyros and Henry were gone. When Leland got home, Myrtle was sitting on the stoop, swishing her stick in the dirt. He eased himself down beside her, rested his elbows on his knees and looked about him. The neighborhood was quiet and hazy. Myrtle's traps hummed in the yard and the alleyway. The sounds of cutlery on plates clinked from windows. Somewhere nearby, a man and woman screamed at each other.

When will they come? Myrtle asked.

Was it his friends or O'Brien she asked about? No matter. Leland thought of O'Brien. His dumb jeering face and his arm-wrestling and his toadies. *They'll probably try to take us by surprise.*

Then we'll be on guard all night, right, Dad?

That's right. Where's your concertina?

Hours came and went. Myrtle played every song she knew, and even Leland hummed along. Later, they sat quiet and listened to the dying-down sounds of the neighborhood. Still no Spyros and Henry. Sometimes Leland got up and walked to the street, looked up and down. But his friends were not to be seen.

Well, girl, he finally said. *Those fellows are cowards.*

Myrtle sighed. *We'll just have to stay here and guard the traps by ourselves, is all.*

Leland rolled up his sleeves. *That's right. You and me can take him on.*

I got my stick.

Let's see you swing it.

She got up and held the stick like a bat, winding up and whooshing it, making a little whistling wind that tickled the hairs on Leland's arms. Her serious eyes and her funny smile. Leland couldn't help but laugh, and Myrtle laughed too, and sat back next to him, and rested her head on his shoulder. Her hair smelled of bug powder.

The sun began to set, and the sky got murky, and a drizzle started, turning the whole yard to mud. The Rag Lady passed with her cart. She held a black umbrella, one corner of it smashed and hitched up to expose a rib. Otherwise, there was no one. The flies had gone wherever flies go when it rains. Leland imagined flies lined up at the bar in a fly-sized pub, each gripping a pint that reflected back in red eyes, watching the rain dash the window. He thought again of Spyros and Henry.

And here they were. Spyros and Henry, both sopping, panting, come up the street and into the yard. Spyros was red and Henry was green. Like Christmas, thought Leland. Runnels of dye dripped off their pant legs and down their wrists.

Did you run here? asked Myrtle. *Your shoe's untied.*

All the way, Missy, said Spyros. He bent down to lace his shoe.

There's some more sticks over there, said Myrtle. She scooted closer to Leland, gestured at them to sit down.

We're not gonna sit around waiting, said Henry. *We already went by O'Brien's house. He's there.*

Spyros put out his red hand. *Let's get him.*

But here was Myrtle's grip, tight on Leland's arm. *He's not going.* She turned to him. *You promised to stay here with me.*

Leland, said Spyros, *don't sit around and wait for him to get organized.*

Later, lying in his bunk or crouched in a reeking trench while exploding shells poxed the night sky, Leland would call up this memory of Myrtle's face. He wanted it to change, to become, somehow, more a little girl's face. To reel backward in time again and tug him right to what he'd felt when she was a newborn. He wanted her to break his heart.

Instead, a woman's scornful look. It was more like Minnie's than anything: zipped-tight mouth, angry flaring eyes. Her hair hung, wet. She said, *Dad, don't leave me,* but her eyes said what Minnie and his other daughters had thought all along: *you're worthless.*

Leland stood and brushed off his damp seat. Myrtle stood too. She yanked at his wrist again and he jerked it away, gripped her shoulders and pushed her back down onto the stoop.

Just you stay here! He picked up her stick, forced it into her hands. Spyros and Henry had already turned away, headed up the street toward Gerrard, where a far-off streetcar keened. He ran to catch up with them. When he took one last look back, Myrtle was only a dark shape on the stoop, head rested on knees, tapping the stick.

Here was O'Brien's house: a slapdash clapboard box on Sackville Street, butted up between two other clapboard houses. It seemed to hold more than one family. A man—not O'Brien—smoked on the porch while a girl, maybe eleven or twelve years old, played solitaire on the floor. One of O'Brien's girls. The red hair and the lizard eyes.

Where's O'Brien? asked Leland.

I'm O'Brien, said the man.

Hell you are, said Henry.

The man butted his cigarette into a saucer on the windowsill. *My cousin's O'Brien, too.*

We want the one works at the leather factory.

The girl ran inside. The man on the porch watched her go, then stared at them in silence. Rain shushed down in waves, sometimes kicking up with the wind and spattering their faces like flying pests.

O'Brien. He stood in the doorframe, his girl peeking out from behind him. He wore a clean change of clothes. His hands and arms were scrubbed pink where he'd rolled up his shirtsleeves. He seemed to smile.

You fellows step one more foot onto my property and my cousin and I'll have to take you out.

We're just here to stop you from coming onto my *property, is all,* said Leland.

What are you talking about, you miserable drunk?

We know what you got planned. This was Spyros. He crossed his arms. *We been told. Maybe your boys is not as loyal as you think.*

You think you can bust my Myrtle's traps? Leland cracked his knuckles.

A confused look on O'Brien's face, curious twist of the brows. He took a couple breaths like to draw air up to his brain. Then, some kind of recognition. He laughed. *And what if I did?*

O'Brien's laugh, such an ugly thing. His teeth seemed oily where his lip curled up, his tongue too red. A boiling in Leland. He wanted to grab that flabby tongue, to rip it out of the stupid skull. He wanted to slam a fist into the ruddy eye sockets, to lift the head by that red hair and slap it home into the mucky ground. Seconds later, he was doing it, pushing his knee into O'Brien's back and socking him in the ear while Spyros and Henry beat on the cousin. The little girl's screams brought her siblings to the yard, and now a whole flock of little O'Briens snatched at Leland and Henry and Spyros, scratching their cheeks and pulling their hair and ripping their bright-colored clothes.

It was about this time, Leland reasoned later, that Effie B's big brothers, the barrel-lifters, made it to his own yard. From what Minnie told him right before she slapped his bruised face and ordered him out of the house, three strapping boys had snuck in the back way and sacked five traps before Myrtle could even swing her stick at them. She'd been all alone, poor girl, though she'd managed to get in a few good blows before they'd pushed her face into the mud, snapped her stick in two, and kicked the rest of her traps to pieces. To finish things off, and just to be extra cruel, they'd smashed her concertina. She'd come in sobbing, soaking wet, with two black eyes, and he didn't dare disturb her now because she'd finally cried herself to sleep.

After Minnie slammed the door behind him, Leland stood outside, aching and stunned and sober. Here was the yard, a disaster. Boot marks in the muck where Myrtle had tangled with the boys. Scraps of wood and mesh. Broken saucers, spilled gizzards and gristle. The bellows from the concertina, torn and stretched and pathetic in the mud, like an exhausted lung. Leland wandered through the scene, a lost man, newly arrived in some unfamiliar world. Could he go back? Was it possible to leap back only an hour, and why not? One trap, knocked over in the skirmish and skidded over against the fence, was left intact. He set it upright.

Leland stood under Myrtle's window, wet clothes sucking at his buttocks and back and belly. One of his eyes was swollen shut where O'Brien had socked him, right before the police whistle, the clatter of footsteps, the mad dash home. It throbbed, now, in time with his heartbeat. Myrtle's black eyes must throb too, he thought. How could a young girl sleep with this kind of pain?

Myrtle, he whispered. He cupped his hands around his mouth and tried again. *Myrtle!*

A face at the window. Not Myrtle, but a younger daughter. *Go away!*

She slapped the window shut. Its pane, old and dirty, still sent back a reflection: a coin of light that was the moon.

The quarter. Leland remembered it with sudden horror. He must have lost it in the fight, somewhere in O'Brien's front yard. It explained everything about this terrible luck. He reached into his pocket to feel the empty place.

And it was there. He drew it out and held it in his palm. Cool and shiny as ever. His Majesty looked dapper in the moonlight, almost King Arthur–like, and Leland hated him as much as he hated O'Brien. He hurled the coin against the side of the house. It dashed off under some bushes. Later, he'd scrape around the place where he thought it had landed. But, right then, he went to sleep in the shed.

Next day, he woke long after work had begun. Don't even bother to show up again if you miss a day, the foreman had said, because some other fellow's got your job. The mud had dried on his clothes, leaving them stiff enough to brush off with his hands as he emerged from the shed, reeking and sweaty.

And there was Myrtle, bruise-faced and limping, headed out for last count with a small tin of what was left of her flies. Leland followed. He called her name, again and again. When she didn't respond, he stayed some paces behind.

He followed her past the familiar shops on Queen Street, the rumbling streetcars and the sharp-shouldered bustlers and the dogs and the zipping flies that seemed especially abundant on this last day of the Swat the Fly Contest.

And here was City Hall, its big brown bell tower and gargoyles and arches, and the robust little swatters dashing up the stairs two at a time. Myrtle took a long time climbing the steps. Leland stood and watched her until she disappeared inside the building. Then, not knowing what else to do, he sat in his usual spot.

Should he have been surprised, in that moment, to see the three big boys toting their sister's whisky barrel while the little girl led the way? They seemed to come out of nowhere and march up the stairs without effort. Leland hurried to his feet, ran at them as best he could on a staircase, yelling that they were done for, they'd pay for what they did to his Myrtle. But the third brother, like some Goliath, shoved him away. He tumbled down a few steps before calling for Officer Ernie, who must have been somewhere else on his patrol, because there was no answer, and everyone stared.

The final count took a long time. When the flycatchers finally emerged, the work day was over and people were headed home, arms hanging from overpacked streetcars. Here was Myrtle. She held the empty tin, and something else. She stopped in front of Leland.

Are you number one? he asked.

Of course I'm not, and I only got five bucks, thanks to you.

Five bucks is better than nothing, said Leland, though he couldn't quite believe it.

You keep it, then. She tossed her prize at him. It bounced off his mucky shirt and landed by his feet: a gold coin. Some fancy piece that looked like it had come from the Royal Mint. Leland had never seen a five-dollar coin before. He tried to polish it with his shirt, held it in his palm. Here again, the face of the King.

He thought he might do the noble thing and keep the coin for Myrtle, slip it under her pillow one night after she'd cooled down. But he knew he wouldn't. He knew he needed it.

Minnie let him back into the house that evening, just as she had every time before, but things were different around home, now that Myrtle ignored him too. The girl's face, when they crossed paths, a cool mask of indifference. There was no music, now, not even humming, and most of the time she was out of the house, working some job, or out somewhere in the neighborhood. Leland could hardly stand the place. Before two months were up, he'd left home for good.

Myrtle must have decided this was the end of her time in the family home too, because Leland heard she was married within the year. Some American kid who took her with him back to Michigan. The Rag Lady told him this news while he haggled with her over the price of his old color-stained work clothes. The whole thing had gone real quick, she said. One day the girl was there, sitting on the stoop, and the next, well, he knew about this kind of marriage, didn't he?

For the next few years, while he did small jobs of work delivering groceries or washing windows or even collecting scraps of tin, he'd sometimes glimpse Minnie or one of the girls somewhere along Queen or Parliament Streets, each going to their own jobs at laundries or sewing in the Eaton's factory. They never seemed to notice him.

In fact, the whole city seemed to hum on without him, to want, even, to rid itself of him. The way it changed, so quick, felt almost like a personal offense, and sometimes he might even stop a fellow on the street to tell him how bad things had become. Every store seemed to have a new sign lit with gaudy bulbs. More and more cars, noisy and coughing smoke. Houses were torn down and new ones built right on the rubble. Even the pubs were closing, and fancy hotels being put in. When war broke out, and he heard able-bodied men were needed in Europe, he lied about his age and found himself dug into a trench in France with boys who weren't even as old as Myrtle.

Maybe that was why he wrote her, one evening while some of his troop played rummy and some wrote letters of their own and one boy close by moaned, pitiful, in his sleep. Leland had run out of his rum ration, but he did have a stumpy pencil and half a sheet of paper. He addressed the letter care of Minnie, and he hoped she'd forward it on, but he doubted Minnie'd even spend the price of a stamp on anything to do with him. He wrote, anyway.

Dear Myrtle,

Here I am in France and I wish I had another sight but this trench. Not even a glimpse of the Eiffel Tower. Sometimes I think I might take my leave and go to see it by myself. Captain here often threatens to discharge me and I hope he does it too.

I've only got a little light left here so I will write until it fades.

I hear you live in the States now and you are married. So both of us has got out of Toronto and I'd say that's for the best. That city will never be a good place. It's always been a stinking garbage hole and probably will be a hundred years.

I think of you some, especially when boys get up singing. Most of the time we have no instruments to accompany us but I hear your concertina always in my mind. Sometimes it strikes up at night too when all the other boys is asleep or even when they tell us we might go over the top my heart starts banging and there's your music right away. I hear all the songs you used to play those days in the parlor like it's my own private concert and aren't the notes beautiful and don't they carry far.

He paused. The tiny pencil ached his fingers.

Love, your Father, he wrote, because the light was gone.

BAD

Sasha wanted to cut a horse's tail. To feel the long swish of it apart from the animal, and swish it, herself, like the wind. When all the other girls were asleep, she snuck out past the tuck shop and the main lodge and the lake and the barn, into the paddock where the camp's horses were kept.

Under the moon, the horses shifted. Caught the edges of the moonlight, so they were just illuminated, then returned to shadow. She followed their soft munching and she trickled her hand along their ticking sides. When she found Niblet, her favorite horse, she knew him by the sweet grassy breath, the round belly, the soft muzzle he worked against her neck.

She wove her fingers through the brittle strands. Niblet let her hold his tail still, let the flies settle on him, just as he'd let her mount him from the wrong side on her first day at camp, let her yank at his bit, let her bring him back to the paddock without picking the dirt that clogged his hooves, let her kiss him wetly on the nose. Niblet was old and had let many girls do many things to him. Once, he'd been returned to the paddock wearing a scarf and a Tilley hat.

She wanted his whole tail. She cut at it from just below where the bone stopped and there was only hair, and the cutting took a long time. The scissors were from the craft cabin. They were gummy, loose at the joints. She worked them through in many slices. Sometimes they jammed, and she pried them apart with both hands. Sometimes strands, plucked by the breeze, slipped from her fingers and skittered across the grass until she lost sight of them. She'd imagined cutting tails in one smooth slice like horses were smooth when they ran, but cutting tails was not such a nice business. Like when she'd cut her dolls' hair, it came out uneven and chopped.

Niblet shuddered. Once, he tried to flick his tail out of her grip, but Sasha recaptured it, and finished the job.

She weighed the tail, the heft and wave of it. She held it and swished it like her own. The soft shush against the summer air. She dangled it like a grass skirt. She held it to the end of her tailbone where it might go, and imagined herself a flowy creature, the beautiful inner machinery that helped her gallop along. Niblet looked at her sideways from where he stood, the remains of his own tail now only a brush that wagged, and let out a sharp sigh.

Sasha tied up each end of the tail with hair elastics pulled from the bottom of her pockets, next to gum wrappers and crumbs. She stretched the elastics almost to breaking. And she carried the tail, slung over her small shoulder, back across the camp. She stuffed it into a duffel bag under her bunk.

Next day, girls came back from their first ride with questions on their faces. Talk of Niblet's tail was all around camp. Mrs. Wills, the camp director, angry and red-faced, gathered everyone together in the dining hall. All the girls were silent. Sasha sat with the other girls in her cabin, all ten or eleven years old, all wearing the same teal tee shirt with two running horses, the same breeches with patched thighs, the same plastic bangles that clicked against each other. They spilled salt on the table and fingered anxious tracings into it as Mrs. Wills told everyone to imagine waking up missing an ear, that this is what it felt like to lose one's tail. To think about how long it takes for horsehair to grow. Years. Longer than Niblet had left to live.

I want the person who did this, said Mrs. Wills, *to come to me, and tell me why.*

There was silence. Sasha heard the deep slub of her own blood. She didn't know why. She didn't know why she'd wanted to cut his tail. She had wanted it; she had taken it. She didn't know why she did the things she did. But she knew, now, she was bad. She wore the tee shirt and the breeches and the bangles, but there was something not like the other girls in her. There was something wrong inside.

All day the other girls in Sasha's cabin talked of horsehair. *What kind of freak would do that? I hope they lose their ear. I hope they die.* That night, lying in bed, their whispers were tail swishings. The tail drummed soft against the underside of Sasha's bunk. Tail-shapes swam on the ceiling.

The next morning, before her first ride, Sasha watched the riding instructors nuzzle and kiss Niblet in the paddock. With kicking heart, she went to him. Binder twine had been braided into the remains of his tail to give him some relief from flies. It slapped his twitchy haunches. He looked like a birthday donkey who'd just been pinned. An instructor with brassy hair and too-tight breeches stroked his long face. His eyes were closed; he was half-asleep.

Poor boy, said the instructor. *Poor old boy. Poor old short tail.*

Sasha had a carrot. She held it out to Niblet, and he took it without hesitation. He nosed against her like nothing had happened. He let her saddle and ride him. After the lesson, she washed and brushed him and picked out his hooves. She wanted him to bite her, to slam her against the end of the stall with a kick. But Niblet breathed on her warmly. He rested his head on her shoulder, so his whiskers tickled her cheek.

She thought of going to Mrs. Wills. Of Mrs. Wills' heavy hands clasped tight in her rumpled khaki lap, how she would say *I'm glad you told me,* but her eyes would glitter, set into her face like stones wedged into mud. Of how maybe Mrs. Wills would give Sasha another chance to be good, make her bus dishes for the rest of camp, or muck out stalls with a gap-pronged rake. Or how maybe she wouldn't, and Sasha's parents would arrive and watch her pack her things while the other girls in her cabin were riding. Then, Sasha would only be an empty bunk, an emptiness that announced her, and maybe the other girls would hold their breath and squeeze their eyes shut as they passed it to avoid breathing in what badness she might have left behind, or maybe they'd smother it in laundry and dusty riding helmets. And maybe later they'd come up to Niblet in the paddock and offer him a carrot. And he'd munch it and let them touch and kiss his soft nose and his graying forehead while his brush-tail slapped at his sides, just as it did now.

Niblet fell asleep as Sasha stroked his velvet ears. She held onto the thought of her confession as best she could, even as the breeze came to take it. Even as it slipped from her clutch, strand by strand, and whirled away.

A GENERAL CONFUSION
OVERTOOK THE
WHOLE VICINITY

Mrs. Jeffries held the article aloft and read in a voice very official.

"The cheapest, best and most agreeable medicine in the world is HASHEESH, The Great Eastern Remedy, Used For Thousands of Years by the Ancient Hindoos, Persians, Jews, Greeks, Chinese, Japanese, Arabians, Egyptians, Chaldeans and the Assyrians."

Rested upon the confectionery counter and under her hand, a tin of Maple Sugar Hasheesh Candy from the Ganja Wallah Hasheesh Candy Company. She drummed its side with her fingernails. Around her, a clot of men and boys, all farmers and farmhands, all quiet and sucking, except when they clacked the candies against their teeth.

"Sacred and profane history alike inform us, says the Reverend John Wesley, that these were the most Beautiful, Happy, Healthy, Cheerful and Long-lived Races of people that ever existed."

She frowned, scanning the rest of the article. Sure Cure for All Sorts of Fevers, it said. Sure Cure for Gout and Excessive

Fatness. Sure Cure for Rheumatism in General. For Dysentery and Summer Complaints. There were so many Sure Cures, too many to list. So many customers had requested the candy that she'd had to get it in special from Springfield, and now she considered the ailments of the men in front of her. Excessive Fatness, yes. Which one had Summer Complaints?

Look here who likes the stuff, said a farmer. He stabbed the article with a finger. "*GEN GRANT SAYS IT IS OF GREAT VALUE.*"

"*For the wounded and feeble,*" *it says,* continued Mrs. Jeffries. *Are you feeble, now?*

Chuckles went around. That farmer sucked his candy with particular relish, giggling. Giggling! A man didn't giggle, not a farmer, but it wasn't unpleasant seeing him draw back his sun-browned lips and expose the gappy teeth. When was the last time a hard-working man just laid down his troubles and giggled, truly tickled by something or another, especially in these times, these trying times? This fellow's son, bless him, only nineteen, was a Union soldier. Just now he was home on leave, and that dear boy was out on the courthouse lawn drinking beer and getting up in song with a bunch of fellow soldiers, all grown up together here in Charleston, all now out there fighting for our very country, dodging minié-balls and cannonballs and heaven knows what other sorts of balls they had flying around on those battlefields. You could hear them singing, just across there.

In fact, wasn't it her job, Mrs. Jeffries, to bring grown men a giggle or two once in a while, with a good book of jokes sold cheap from the twirling rack on her countertop or a plug of tobacco brought in from Chicago or even from little candies, why not? Sometimes she made chocolate candies or fudge in a kettle over the fire, but more often now people wanted what was sold in the big city stores or carried by soldiers. Necco wafers, horehound, sticks of peppermint. If the Ganja candy was the balm that restored a man's soul it must be good, and look, now, how the men were laughing! All of them, hawing and gasping, clapping each other on the back, laughing just to see each other.

Amanda, said Mrs. Jeffries.

Her daughter looked up from sweeping. The men laughed at this.

We'll make another big order of these.

She raised the tin and all the men cheered. Amanda only knotted up her mouth into a little frown, rolled her eyes. She was of that age, that disagreeable age.

BUT! Announced another man, this one a farmhand from Lerna, a new boy just home from battle with some actual war wound no one talked about.

He stabbed the same article, pointing to an endorsement from "*GEN LEE, THE CONFEDERATE GENERAL.*" It seemed all present pictured that man, clothed in gray and wearing a hat of gray and riding a big gray horse that set off his gray whiskers, stopped right in front of them, right there in the middle of the store just about where Amanda stood daydreaming with her chin resting on the broom handle, to solemnly declare that he wished to place a Dollar Tin of the HASHEESH CANDY in the pocket of every Confederate Soldier, for he was convinced it alleviated suffering.

This candy don't take no sides!

Well! Said another. He plucked the candy wet from his mouth and examined it, like he could gaze in it all the action in the Eastern Theater.

Some men grumbled and clicked their candies with more vigor, a little agitation rising in the group.

Don't pay no mind to advertisements, admonished Mrs. Jeffries. *All they want is to sell. That's just business. You got to sell to*

people you love and people you just can't even stand. Isn't that right,
Amanda?

But Amanda made no answer. She stared, now, out the window at the commotion on the courthouse yard, where yelling and screaming had started up. A clutch of Union boys, all
drunk, struggled against a throng of country men while other
folks scattered to every corner of the square.

That's Bryant Thornhill, said a candy-sucking farmer, who
took the liberty, now, of clutching Amanda's shoulder with
talon-like grip, leaning close enough to the window to fog it.
Other candy-suckers crowded around him.

Bryant Thornhill, a name everyone knew: troublemaker,
always stirring something up. When he was just a boy Mrs.
Jeffries used to catch him stuffing rock candy into his pockets
or nicking squares of fudge. As a man, now, he was no different.
He wore a rough flapping coat and wide-brimmed hat in imitation of a Confederate soldier, with flashing pistol at his hip
which he drew, waved like a mad pirate, and fired into the air.

Amanda gripped her broom, white-knuckling it, while the
candy-sucking men drew up to the window, pressing their
hands flat against the panes. Bryant Thornhill had followers:
other men from Westfield and Mattoon and Paris, all in thin,
flapping jackets, many on horseback. Some young boys you
might see loading bales onto wagons in hay season. Some old
men with long and yellowed beards. All their faces familiar
but not family-close: people you'd see at fairs and festivals, at
community gatherings or on the square doing whatever business had brought them to town. Buying a new hat, maybe.
With a bandage knotted around their heads, nursing an ab-
scess, come for a rare visit to the dentist. Those sorts of people.
Some had two, three, four pistols hitched to their belts. Some
held the collars of Union soldiers and punched and punched
and punched.

Shots went up all around, now, and a general confusion overtook the whole vicinity. Judges and lawyers and plaintiffs and defendants streamed out of the courthouse, pursued by Thornhill's men, and followed by the Sheriff, who whinnied in excitement and waved his own pistol overhead before he fired at the retreating judges, felling one instantly. He was Thornhill's man, too.

All this too much for the candy-suckers, some of whom clung to Mrs. Jeffries while others cowered behind Amanda's skirt or made cries more like the wails of goats than anything. The farmer whose son was among those under attack stood crying, tears tumbling into his rusty beard. All of them frozen in place.

What was she to do, Mrs. Jeffries, in a mess such as this? Never did she imagine she'd see any of the war, not up close, especially owing to Mr. Jeffries' being unfit for service, having lost his foot years ago in Kentucky. Bless that foot, wherever it is, she'd thought to herself. A disgraceful, secret thought.

Here came a man from somewhere out on the street. He snatched open the door and stood panting in the doorway, shirt open at the collar, stained with someone's blood. Everyone, even the candy-suckers, dread silent.

For God's sake, said the man. *Give me a pistol!*

A pistol? Mrs. Jeffries, looking helpless around at the candy-suckers. At Amanda, who looked helpless back at her. She still held the tin of Maple Sugar Hasheesh Candy from the Ganja Wallah Hasheesh Candy Company, which rattled, now, in the shaking hand she offered. The man grimaced.

And he was gone, run back toward the gunfire. The door swung closed, its bell jingling merrily.

Oh Lord, save us! cried a farmer, who had fallen to his knees.

There comes a time in every woman's life when she is called upon to do extraordinary things. Mrs. Jeffries' mother, for instance, had saved her own son from drowning in the Ohio River by swimming in after him and lifting the boy to safety on a passing raft. She'd been unable to save herself, weighted down, as she was, by her waterlogged dress, and her nine-year-old daughter had watched from the riverbank as her mother's head disappeared under water for the last time.

Now, Mrs. Jeffries feared her own time to do extraordinary things had come. The creepy feeling of destiny was over her: a tingling of the arms and the back of the neck. And here was her own daughter, wailing, flanked by a throng of paranoid farmers, all watching this unfold on the square: two young men, one Union and one anti-, caught in a life-and-death struggle. Both uncommon handsome, with what Mrs. Jeffries sometimes referred to as the beautiful jaw, both evidently known to Amanda, who was in agonies. One farmer fanned the girl with his hat while another held steady the broom she used to brace herself.

Both young men were on the ground, now, and the Confederate boy was on top, choking the Union. How bright the young soldier's face as he struggled for breath: candy-red, a dipped apple. Amanda only shouted, *Eli! Eli! No!* while tears came down her cheeks. Her look, very beautiful and tragic and just a picture of suffering. Much prettier than she'd ever been before, and womanly, too—it got you right here.

Well, this was enough. If Eli should mean something to dear Amanda—Eli! A strong name! Mrs. Jeffries had wondered when Amanda might take interest in a man, and here was bright red Eli, her future son-in-law—then Eli must live. Armed with new resolve, Mrs. Jeffries threw open the door to the confectionery, admitting the pop and whistle of gunfire and the odor of gunpowder and horse manure and whiskey. For just a moment, the whole world seemed to pause around her.

But—praise the Lord!—Eli was on top now, by way of

some maneuver he must have learned in the army. Now he punched the daylights out of the Confederate boy, punched and punched and punched. Each punch igniting an explosion of pride in Mrs. Jeffries as she watched from the doorway. Eli! Eli!

Caleb! Oh no, Caleb!

Amanda again, clasping her hands to her heart.

Caleb?

Ma'am, said the farmer who fanned Amanda with his hat. *The fella underneath yonder.* He gestured toward the window with a quick flash of his eyes.

Caleb. The Confederate boy. With each punch to his left temple, Caleb's head yanked dangerously to the right, like it might just pop off at any minute. And, with each blow, a new cry from Amanda, who moaned, now, that *he's gonna kill him, he's gonna kill him.*

A Confederate militiaman in the family. It might not wash with polite society here in Central Illinois, though family back in Kentucky would embrace the marriage. Mrs. Jeffries supposed she and Mr. Jeffries could send the young couple away, secret, to Lexington, and they could live a very nice life there, trading horses, maybe, and living in a handsome house with a veranda— oh, the verandas of her youth!—where Amanda could sit out on a rocking chair with her babies and just rock them to sleep. To be sure, there's nothing like a Kentucky veranda.

But, still. Eli sure was showing Caleb. Of course, violence was distasteful—*of course*—but, being raised Southern, Mrs. Jeffries couldn't help but admire a man who could throw a good punch. And couldn't Eli punch with style? Her own mother had always said, *A gentleman can throw punches while he sweats in his jacket.* Or was it *A gentleman can gouge out an eye without losing his hat?* And, look: he kept his hat on the whole time.

Well, said Mrs. Jeffries. *Which do you want?*

Amanda sobered. Her look, a widening of the eyes, like to underline how utterly stupid her mother, how little the woman understood of love, and how very special her own feelings and inner thoughts. No one had ever had them before.

I! Don't! Know!

But Mrs. Jeffries *did* understand love. If Amanda had to know, she understood better than anyone that losing two people you loved was likely to be ten times worse than losing one. Now she was out in the street, dodging spooked horses and shoppers running for cover and drunks who'd stumbled out of the saloons on Whiskey Row. She cleared a volley of gunfire that had broken out between two crowds of men, clutching her skirt away from her fast feet. She glanced back at the confectionery: there were the farmers, folded around the open doorway, anxiously calling her to come back, come back. Amanda stood in their midst, eyes wet and glowy.

Now Mrs. Jeffries gained the courthouse yard, where Eli still punched Caleb. Each blow made a noise very unpleasant, like a wet pumpkin falling off the back of a wagon. Between blows, Caleb writhed, one hand impotently scratching at his side. This is what she would do: come running at the pair, throw all her weight, and knock the boys apart. She took a stance she'd seen little children take at the County Fair before they ran foot races, one leg braced behind, one crooked forward at the knee. In the hand that hiked up her skirts, the tin of hasheesh candy, which rattled like her own tiny drummer.

Mrs. Jeffries charged. Gaining speed, she locked eyes on the brawling pair. She aimed right for Eli, who failed to notice the pistol Caleb finally produced from the holster at his side, lifted to Eli's beautiful jaw and—time unbearable slow, now, as Mrs. Jeffries hurtled toward this disaster—shot him, bullet blasting his Union cap right off where it tore through the back of his skull.

No time to stop the collision: Mrs. Jeffries and the body of Eli tumbled two, three times together before resting against a beer barrel. Eli, limp and heavy, laid with his bleeding head on her lap: a child. A heavy, sleeping, faceless child, empty eyes staring at nothing, empty head void of dreams. The impulse to comfort him, to find the scattered parts of him and piece him back together. That would make everything better. Handsome Eli. Mrs. Jeffries looked down on the mangled face. She looked and looked and looked.

Only screaming could shake her from that private moment: a chorus of farmers, screaming in a higher register than she'd ever heard before, and the wails of Amanda, carrying across the street like a loose ribbon.

Caleb was up, stumbling. His head lolled on his neck, which he rubbed as if he'd just awoken from a deep and restful sleep. His whole body was dusted in the dirt of the courthouse lawn—rust brown—and, when he turned to see what he'd done to Eli, he squinted through eyeholes swollen near-shut, his nose broken and bleeding, his beautiful jaw now knocked to one side. He opened his mouth to breathe; he had no front teeth. He tested this new and tender void with a curious tongue.

No notice of Mrs. Jeffries, who gently pushed Eli aside and rose, shaky, using the barrel to brace herself. Caleb seemed only to follow some animal instinct, turning toward a noise or a movement, pistol dangling from his fist. Unclear whether he could see at all. He snorted up a gob of blood and phlegm and spat at his feet.

But, he could hear. The voice of Amanda, the only female voice in a wash of gunfire and guttural yells: *What did you do? What did you do?*

He craned his head forward, like that gesture might eke open his swollen eyeholes enough to glimpse Amanda in the doorway, to keep her locked in his sights as he tottered this way and that across the street, now stumbling into the path of an oncoming cart, now just missing it, now glancing the shoulder of a fellow crossing the other way. Caleb raised his pistol to the fellow, who threw his hands up and backed off. Then he turned back toward the door to the confectionery. Toward Amanda, whose look of horror said everything.

Where did Mrs. Jeffries get the speed? She was running again, faster, now, than she'd ever run before. Dress weighted with blood, sucking at the fronts of her legs, pulling her down, down toward Eli. Still she pushed ahead, lungs prickling against the current of the street and dust and wind that kicked up. She pushed ahead of Caleb, who loped toward the door to the confectionery, swinging his gun. Like Caleb, she, too, kept her eyes on Amanda, who looked to her mother like she had as a little girl: needful and afraid, arm outstretched. *Come back, please come back.*

Amanda in Mrs. Jeffries' arms, burying head against neck. The girl shook. The floor of the confectionery shook. Everyone shook. While Mrs. Jeffries had been tackling Eli, the farmers had got into a second tin of hasheesh candy and some licorice twists, and they all sucked furiously, now, quaking and sucking and clicking.

Here he comes!

Caleb, almost up at the door. Everyone looked on him: the shiny-swollen eyes and the burst lips and the knocked-aside jaw. The smears of sweat and dirt, and the bloody knuckles joined to the fingers that held the pistol, the outrageously shiny pistol. The blown-away face of Eli loomed up. Here was the man who did that violence.

For the rest of her life Mrs. Jeffries would remember herself, in this moment, firing the shot that struck Caleb somewhere deep in his gut. Untrue, of course—the imaginings of a superstitious old woman, Amanda would say, it was only a stray bullet from someone out on the street—but, all the same, Mrs. Jeffries asked God a favor in that moment and, for the first time in her whole life, it seemed, God heard her in that very moment and asked no questions, only put a gun in her hand, a terrifying gun forged in His armory—and there was Caleb, gutshot, hunched, with a glassy look of surprise, just like he'd been tapped on the shoulder. He reared up, touched something on his back: his hand came away bloody. He looked at that blood for a long, long time. Behind him, a farmer hurried his oxen down the street, shielding himself from the melee with a floppy straw hat. Dust smoked the sky.

Another thing Mrs. Jeffries would remember: a gutshot man could walk on for a while before he dropped. Long enough, for instance, to cross the threshold of a confectionery and stand among a stunned gathering of candy-sucking farmers. Caleb shuffled in, feet dragging. Stopped right in the middle of the room. Blood bloomed on the back of his shirt. His breaths came wet and bubbly. His gaze wandered from person to person, like to find someone he knew. Each averted their eyes. Amanda approached him, went right up to his face, searched it, and repeated his name. Worked the pistol out of his hand finger-by-finger, gently, gently, and dropped it on the floor. He paid no mind.

Why, now, did he look right past Amanda, straight at Mrs. Jeffries? A moment she didn't ask for, didn't want at all. Not after what he'd done to Eli, this boy—boy. That's what he was. A boy who killed. Watery, pleading eyes buried deep in his swollen face. She'd seen this look before, long ago, worn—no,

43

she didn't want to think this, wouldn't think it—worn by her small brother when he'd been paddled back to shore looking choked and purple like a newborn baby, delivered to the river-bank where she stood, a little girl, suddenly his sole guardian. He'd stood there not even knowing he'd killed his own mother. Here's what she knew: he was five years old, he looked to her for something, and—she hated him.

And here was all she had to offer this boy, Caleb: the tin of Maple Sugar Hasheesh Candy from the Ganja Wallah Ha-sheesh Candy Company, still in her grasp. The tin dented, its contents broken and powdery. She took Caleb's hand, lifted it—the surprising weight of it, palm up—into a cup-shape, and poured the candy. Take some. Take all of it.

Caleb, with some difficulty, lifted the shaking hand to his toothless mouth and tumbled the candy inside. Nothing to look at, now, but the puckered lips and bloodied cheeks, heaving in and out as he sucked, like a horrific baby falling asleep at mother's breast. All gathered around to view this phenomenon, but Mrs. Jeffries already knew what was next.

Now he'd sucked the candies down to half their size, his eyes beginning to glaze.

Now he stared off at the kind of future none of them could see.

Now, worst of all, he smiled.

MACHINES OF
ANOTHER ERA

Many years later, after he'd forgotten how to write stories, García Márquez began to call his brother. *What day is it?* he would ask. And his brother would tell him, in a voice that blended respect and simple tones, *it is Tuesday,* or *it is Friday afternoon,* or *it is the last Monday morning in October.*

It got to be that he called his brother several times a day. His brother would stretch the telephone cord to sit in a croaking wicker chair behind his house, where the vegetables in the garden strained their skins with ripeness. Each conversation was another question. Once, García Márquez phoned to ask what their grandmother was preparing for dinner. His brother, already seventy-five years old and the younger of the two, struggled with the question. Doña Alexandra was dead forty years. But, also, he saw her spirit in the garden. Saw it more often, now that García Márquez was slipping away. She was there now, as they talked. He watched her slide her bracelets up her crepe arms to pluck the ingredients from his own vegetable patch: green peppers, tomatoes, beans that curled from their stalks. He repeated these ingredients to his brother. *Ah*, said García Márquez. *She is making an omelet.*

García Márquez's brother would often lie in bed with his balcony doors open, and let the night shapes swim across his ceiling and the street sounds tread the room, and follow his sadness as far as it took him. García Márquez, so quiet, but possessed of such beautiful imagination, was slipping away. And he, who loved facts and figures, who knew himself to have no imagination, could only stand by and observe. His own students at the university had often asked more about his sibling than about cell structure. And he always admitted he knew little of his brother's magic, of how the stories came to him, and from what source, and when they would come again.

García Márquez's questions continued until they were so pure and so wide they might be asked by a child. How long was the day, and what creature dropped the rains, and women with long skirts: did they float? His brother gave simple, factual answers, that slipped from García Márquez's memory like water through sand. The answer to *Where do dogs come from* left García Márquez sounding perplexed, until his brother heard the receiver slip from a hand and clatter against the floor. Next came the voice of García Márquez's wife. *He is too tired to speak anymore.*

What comfort can a brother give to a disappearing brother? His students looked on from their tiered desks: their floating faces, pale and indistinct. Doña Alexandra, sitting in his own wicker chair, offered no consolation but gave him a silvery look. Her ringed hand stroking her favorite cat.

The night shapes, blue and dusk and black, the sound of the street, sleeplessness. A bedside lamp flicked amber against midnight. García Márquez's brother, reading a work by García Márquez. In the fiction, the comfort of emerald leaves, and rare birdsong. Telegraph and carriage: the machines of another era. The bitter tastes of wine and pickles and rich wet earth, gritty and specked with life. Alchemy. Ice. Clothes on the line. Soft and vengeful spirits that wandered among the living. A child born with a hundred years' wisdom. An old man with black and tattered wings.

The telephone, at this unearthly hour, ringing at his bedside. It was García Márquez, he was sure, though all he could hear on the other end was uneven breath. Neither caller nor answerer spoke for a while. The house trembled, as it sometimes did, and he could hear distant hanging pots chime against each other, their dull music his instruction.

He lifted the book. He began to read aloud. The words, tumbling like moths into the night, lighting on walls and windowsills and fluttering away. The telephone, sturdy against the pouch of his cheek. The uneven breathing on the other end of the line that seemed to say, *I'm listening. Continue.* He did. This familiar story, made new and shapeful by his voice.

When he was finished reading, morning light pricked the edges of the city. There was another moment of breathing. He watched a domestic canary wearing a blue ribbon settle on his balcony railing, preen, and launch itself away. There was a *click,* and there was the long wail of the dial tone. He eased himself from his bed and shut off his lamp. He dressed for the day. He went downstairs.

He ate the omelet Doña Alexandra had prepared for him, that sat waiting at his place at the table.

HELENA, MONTANA

Goodyear's mailbag cried. A ribbon of wails that spooled from the bag's sagging mouth where it sat on the floor of the post office, among two other sagging mailbags. When Goodyear arrived that morning to pick up his deliveries, his coworkers Jones and Bilson, each belonging to a mailbag, slurped from tin cups, leaned on the counter, frowned at him as if to say, *why didn't you get here sooner? Can't you quiet your mail?*

He approached the mailbag. Inside: a package wrapped with butcher paper, personal letters addressed in handwriting he recognized from a long history of correspondence, a catalog of undergarments enveloped in a modest paper sleeve, a baby girl. Her turnip-shaped head, her wet blue eyes, her tear-stained cheeks, her sagging diaper. She sat upright and smashed her fists against her bowlegs. She looked at Goodyear. She crumpled her forehead. She seemed to ask a question: *What are you going to do now, strange man?*

And he must have seemed a very strange man to her: skinny, knock-kneed and bald were it not for his mailman's cap—much like a baby, himself. Taller than Jones or Bilson. So tall that, with upstretched arm, he could reach the top shelf of ingoing/outgoing letters. And frozen in time: not wrinkled or silvery but no longer young, as if he waited for the next part of himself to arrive.

Goodyear lifted the baby. Set her on the counter. She wore a simple smock and a beige hand-knit sweater, pilled all over, with old food crusted into it in spots, and a coal smudge on the sleeve. Her small pockets held her belongings, all sized to lodge tight in a baby's esophagus: a tattered orange hair ribbon, a silver perfume phial yanked from a chatelaine, the lid off a gentleman's flask, a ticket stub for the Chippewa County Fair, a cat's black whisker, a pewter die-cast sheep the size of Goodyear's fingertip. He examined each and set it on the counter, and the baby watched this process with the curious detachment of one who'd passed through many strange hands. She wore a tag, pinned to her back and covered in stamps. She was postmarked Helena, Montana, and here she was in Swansea, Ontario, more than seventeen hundred miles away.

This baby, thought Goodyear, had seen more than he'd ever see in his life.

Not smelling too rosy, said Bilson.

Diaper needs changing, said Jones, who'd fathered so many children that he knew just when a kid was hungry and just when it was tired, and sometimes homed in on moments of conception deep in the guts of women in neighboring houses, back alleys and barns. They sounded, he'd once said between sips from the same tin cup, like a mouse's eek.

I don't know, said Goodyear. He looked at the baby. She raised her scrunched fist to her lips. *She's a parcel. Do we change parcels?*

Bilson furrowed his brow. *That might be tampering. You've already tampered.* He pointed at the perfume phial, the ticket stub, the whisker, the sheep. Goodyear swept the knickknacks into his palm and stuffed them back into the baby's pocket.

Goodyear hoisted the baby in his mailbag, her turnip-head peeking out the top, sometimes a doughy arm pointing. He would walk his usual route. He would tread the path he always trod, stout brick roads and shushing summer trees.

But, the baby. The address pinned to her sweater was for the least favorite house on his route. One whose mailbox he stuffed with bills from various creditors, whose only real letters were sodden and bent at the corners, sometimes stamped at the wrong end. When Goodyear got out between the trees and the road and Jones and Bilson went in their own directions, he tasted worry and looked down at the baby, who looked back up at him.

She was calm. She pointed the way with a fat arm. He followed.

Goodyear was worn out from sleeplessness. He had no baby at home, but he did have a wife whose teeth were going blue—*blue!*—from whatever sickness roiled inside her. She kept him up. She snatched at his collar in the night. She woke, from fever dreams, in a sea of sweat. Her eyes were set back in her skull, now. Too far back, thought Goodyear. Her eyes were halfway out the door. But, now, the sun stroked Goodyear's shoulders, and the weight of the baby swayed pleasantly at his side. Goodyear began to hum. This was happiness: feeling his own feet thump the ground, feeling the warm breathing body that cooed at his hip.

The first delivery was a package, placed into the hands of a young boy playing with tin soldiers on his veranda. He was drawn only to the baby. His sticky fingertips on the baby's soft cheek.

Why's she in your bag? He squinted up at Goodyear.

Goodyear shrugged. *She's a parcel*, he said.

Oh, said the boy. He fumbled with the package's paper edge. He took a breath. *No she's not. She's a baby.* He pinched his nose. *She smells like a baby.*

Babies can be parcels. Goodyear fought the urge to shove the little boy away from the baby, to slap the boy's pinching hand from her arm, where it left red welts. The baby didn't cry.

The boy looked around for a long time. The yard and the street were quiet but for birds. *Can I be a parcel?*

Goodyear imagined walking with this boy, or—worse—carrying the ridiculous weight of him in his satchel. And the constant questions.

No, he said.

Why's she get to be a parcel and not me?

Her mum and dad paid for her postage.

How do you *know?*

There was no answer for this. Still, the boy stared and waited. Goodyear fumbled for a response while watching the baby, with a pickpocket's hand, ease a tin soldier out of the boy's overalls pocket. She tucked it into her smock.

I'm going to ask my mum to mail me, said the boy. He started for the door, then turned back and raised a finger. *Don't move!*

Goodyear moved. He moved off the veranda and out of the yard and down the street, until he heard the boy's cries and quick footfall, and ducked behind a hedge. The boy came ripping past him, yelling, *Mailman! Mailman!* and waving a roll of stamps. He waited until the awful sounds were gone.

But the boy was right: the baby was not a package. Goodyear thought this as he walked on. He thought it as he wedged the second package behind a storm door and the baby laughed at a skittering June bug. He thought it as the smell of her wafted over to a cluster of old men, whose faces puckered like old potatoes.

Everyone seemed old, now that he carried the baby. A carriage clopped by and the horses were old, their eyes bagged and milky, their coats dull as felt hats.

He glanced down to see if the baby was watching the horses. She was, without enthusiasm. She worked her mouth and furrowed her serious brow. As if she'd seen a thousand horses. As if she'd seen every horse.

The letters were for two brothers who'd lived together longer than Goodyear had been alive. They were from the same sender, written in the same script. It was possible they were identical copies of the same letter, though Goodyear would never stray from his duties to steam open the envelopes, or to hold them up to the sun and squint. Goodyear gave one to the baby to turn over and over in her hands as they neared the squat duplex the brothers owned, that crouched behind a thatch of trees. Before he touched the mailbox the baby reached out and lifted its lid, deposited her letter with the poise of a secretary. A baby who knew how to mail a letter! Something surged in Goodyear. He had felt it many years before, when his future wife had burrowed her small hand in his, pointed at two ducks that skimmed Grenadier Pond and said, *They look married.* He'd been walking with her every Tuesday afternoon for the past year-and-a-half, arriving at her doorstep, greeting her parents who nodded politely but without enthusiasm as this lanky, balding mailman took their daughter's arm and led her down High Park Boulevard. And he had waited a year-and-a-half of Tuesdays, gazing at this small woman nearly ten years his junior: the pleasing point of her widow's peak and the milky dome of her forehead and her eyelashes soft as moth wings, waiting for a sign of her affection. Waiting for the ducks.

He gave the baby the catalog of undergarments to hold as he walked. For a moment, he worried she might peel off its sleeve, but she looked ahead. The baby had no interest in undergarments. The baby had a downright Christian attitude, thought Goodyear. The baby offered the catalogue, and Goodyear dropped it into the doctor's mailbox. Quick, the doctor was at the mailbox scooping up the catalog before his wife or anyone took it. He twisted it in his long hands. He inspected the baby.

Not yours? He looked at Goodyear with suspicion.

She's a parcel, said Goodyear, though he didn't believe it. He hitched the mailbag up on his shoulder and looked down at the baby, who was now face-to-face with the squatting doctor. The doctor waved one finger in front of her face and she followed it. The doctor pinched her cheek and inspected the color of her eyelids.

Dehydrated. Overheated, said the doctor. With medicinal hands he removed the baby's sweater, still pinned with the address and stamps, and folded it away in the mailbag. He sniffed. *And needs changing.*

But she's a parcel? Said Goodyear. *Would that be tampering?*

She must've been tampered with a great deal if she's made it this far, said the doctor.

Why hadn't Goodyear thought of this? Of the other mailmen who'd carried the baby on their hips, swung her in their mail bags, hoisted her into sacks and chairs, fed her from their waxed paper lunches, covered her with blankets as she slept? Goodyear was not special. He was only the last person in a long chain of people. Everything he touched, he thought, was dangerously close to the end of its journey.

This was the first time Goodyear had been jealous of another mailman. Even when Bilson was assigned the prime route, dogless, that wound under tall elms, Jones stomped the floorboards and splashed gritty coffee on a package from Sears Roebuck. Goodyear didn't get jealous. But, now, well. The baby reached out and honked the doctor's nose. The doctor scooped her out of the mailbag and held her, let her reach into his pocket and take a cotton swab, let her examine it before tucking it into her smock.

Goodyear thought of her final destination and his stomach leaped.

But he walked on. Duty pulled him along his route, no matter what he felt. Sometimes it guided him gently and sometimes, like today, it dragged him with a rough hand. The baby leaned back in her mailbag sling, like a queen reclined in her litter. And here was the terrible outline of her future as it loomed up from below: the peeling house, the crumbling chimney belching out its oily curl of smoke.

It was worse than he'd remembered.

Goodyear had never seen the person who lived in that gnarled stumpy house, but now he scrutinized their dry garden dotted with doll limbs and spent matchboxes and curious lengths of string, their unswept walkway ruddy with decayed leaves, their greasy windows and their gate that never latched. Today, a squirrel gnawed maniacally on a paint-stripped fencepost. Goodyear tiptoed into the yard. A tiny ribcage cracked under his shoe.

The front door was shut tight against the warm afternoon. Everything was still. Even the coil of smoke above the chimney seemed slowed almost to stopping. Goodyear stood in the yard for a long while, longer than politeness and duty allowed. There was the scritch of squirrel teeth on wood.

And there was a silhouette by the window. Goodyear could only just make out the stooped shoulders, the matted hair and knobby hands. They clutched something that might have been a broom handle but might also have been a thigh bone. The figure seemed to swing this tool. Panic needled Goodyear's heart. He looked down at the baby.

The horror of this: as if some awful bond was between them, the baby raised a pointed finger to the silhouette.

Goodyear hitched the mailbag up on his shoulder. He clasped the baby's bottom like to hold her close to him, releasing the perfume of dirty diaper.

Squeak of un-oiled door hinges; the rasp of dead leaves pushed off the stoop. The figure in the doorway: a girl, perhaps sixteen. She wore a man's old work sweater over a lumpen day dress. Goodyear noticed the shoes: formerly black oxfords, gray now, one toe flapping open to reveal holes in a dingy stocking, her foot kicking back a rangy mutt. She coughed wetly into her sweatered sleeve: a cough that shuddered her whole body, that announced its contagion. When she drew her sleeve away, it showed a spot of bright blood. Goodyear's own stomach leaped to his throat. She worked forward at an agonizing pace, dragging her feet, while the baby agitated the mailbag, tugged at its strap and watched the girl's approach. The open doorway behind the girl was dark and empty, but a sound came from it: the cry of an infant. Two infants? An echo? And, worse: the *cough* of an infant. The girl's wet cough, made miniature, made desperate. Goodyear stood, frozen, nursing his bad feeling. What was coming toward him felt terrible, inevitable—this, the feeling of home.

The girl came close enough to touch. She had a smell. Burning plastic, perhaps, or naphthalene. She pressed her small red hand to her heart, and Goodyear resisted this gesture, its soft feeling. There was no use, he decided, in seeing her face. There was no use knowing more about her as he delivered her package, did the thing he was duty-bound to do. But, the face. It lingered, pulled Goodyear's gaze. A well-drawn mouth. Striking sapphire eyes against her ghosty skin and bright burning cheeks. Mailman and girl breathed heavily. Their breaths threaded together in the air between them. Goodyear girded up baby and bag. He had never strayed from his duties, no, but it was clear, this time, that the delivery address was a mistake—

that the postal system had made a terrible mistake, yes, and that this package belonged with him until such time as the proper recipient could be located, or perhaps—outrageous thought—he was the proper recipient. Perhaps he knew best for this package.

Hello, said the girl.

Electric fear in Goodyear. Why hadn't he expected her to speak to him?

The girl gazed after Goodyear as he backed away, stumbled over the celluloid body of a doll, went out the swinging gate and slapped it to. With kicking heart, Goodyear looked back at the girl, at the moon-pale face. Something tight and aching there. Something that had loomed up before, those times he was quiet and still. He knew, somehow, he would see face again, though he couldn't think of it now, pushed the knowledge away.

This was how he veered from his route: with dashes that scissored lawns' grassy lips. When he reached his own house, he turned quick into the gate and sprinted through the yard and did not stop until they were safe inside the foyer. The hum of his own blood retreated. Then, the house was soft with blue shadows. Its musk was camphor and old rosy sprays of Bellodgia. Somewhere, a clock tocked and the plumbing shuddered. There was also the howl of his wife.

The baby whipped her head around looking for the source. She hooked her tiny fingers through one of Goodyear's belt loops to hoist herself up. When she saw nothing, she arched her back and began to howl, herself: a howl that reeled upstairs to tangle with his wife's. The baby teetered and Goodyear snatched her up, squished her to his chest. She wriggled against his hug, pushing away from him. Her wriggling brought up her stench. Goodyear had never handled a diaper before. With timid hand, he lifted her smock; she was thick with diapers. Layers of clean ones like onion skins fastened with gleaming pins over the soggy inner mess. Maybe he could handle this, but he didn't know how to stop her howling. She wriggled until Goodyear thought he might drop her. He sat her down on the floor where, with quivering chin, she pinched the pewter sheep from her pocket and stared into its face.

What is that?

His wife stood at the top of the stairs. Her yellowed nightie hung on her, sail-like, and she hung on the banister, humped and exhausted, like a woman much older than herself. Her hair fell down in tangles. Even in this dark, Goodyear saw her squint.

That's a baby, she said. She took a rattling breath. She started down the stairs like a wheelbarrow about to pitch over. Goodyear rushed to help her, but she brushed his help away. He followed her down to the sobbing and watched her scoop the baby up into brittle arms. He worried she might break under the baby's weight, but she hoisted her easily. He smelled her sour odor braid with the baby's as she rocked her. Until the baby stopped crying. Until the baby rested her head on his wife's sharp shoulder, and sighed.

His wife turned to him, jiggling the baby. Her face was old leather, but these were the young olive eyes he'd fallen for, watching him now after many years.

What's her name? she asked.

Goodyear thought of the baby's tag. There was no name; just postage stamps. Just a destination, and a return address in Helena, Montana.

Helena, he said.

She smiled. *Helena,* she said to the baby. The baby blew an orb of spit, maybe in response.

And Goodyear watched as his wife stepped out of herself. He followed her, this woman now impossible as when they first met, as she went easily about the house, changing and bathing Helena, singing soft songs, boiling and mashing carrots that she spooned into the baby's mouth, helping her sip warmed milk from a juice glass, swiping dust from the sills and the mantel, where Goodyear never cleaned. When she sang, her voice was clear—not the rusty scrape he was used to—and she smiled for the first time in—how long? He didn't know. Her teeth still blue, but blue like moonlight spilled across water. Goodyear remembered the woman he had guided under the oak and the pine in High Park those years ago: a doughy woman with wide hips and plush breast, with soft hair done in rag curls, with pink complexion and full complement of eyelashes that swatted her cheeks.

Before him now, she held Helena on her hip and looked at him as she had that day on Grenadier Pond. He saw the ducks.

And he saw himself, in the early days of their marriage. How helpless he was; he'd only realized it after their union. The deep ache he'd felt when she'd gone to visit family in Windsor, or even on particularly long mail runs. The way she'd finished a ramekin of mashed potatoes with a thick pat of butter; the way she'd warmed their socks on the radiator; the tough rasped skin on her fingertips: how simple. How afraid he'd been to need her, then.

Sit with me? he asked.

She sat on the sofa and bounced Helena on her lap, humming softly. He sat beside her and circled her shoulders with his arm. When he pulled her in close she was still bones and sinew and vinegar smell. He pushed this back in his mind, to where he pushed all unpleasant things. To where he pushed the truth about Helena. To where he pushed the girl who waited for her. But the truth would not stay hidden. The truth busted its way out and he clutched after it like a slipped bar of Pears.

She's a package, he said.

His wife laughed. *She looks like a baby to me.*

She was in my mailbag this morning. With stamps.

His wife lifted Helena to her feet and stared into the serious face. *You can mail a baby?* As if she were asking the baby. Helena smiled, all gums. For the first time, she seemed to know nothing. She had no answers.

Goodyear's wife turned to him. The room was unlit, but he had no trouble seeing her worry. He knew this look, too. The same look she wore when the doctor had first leaned over her with wrinkled brow, had first looked back at him, had first shaken his head. It was the same look the girl had worn, as he'd pulled the baby out of her reach.

Was she addressed to us? she asked. She seemed to smudge, just slightly, like a figure in a watercolor.

There was a long silence. The thing to do in this moment, thought Goodyear, was to hold her close as long as he could. To memorize this blink of happiness already gone, to take into himself every detail of her frail, tremoring body as it let go of its last good feeling. He took her thin wrist in his hand; it was cold, but he held it.

He looked down to where Helena had reached over and grasped a bright button on his mailman's jacket. To where she yanked the button away with a tug, turned it over a moment in her hands, and tucked it into her pocket, out of sight, among her other treasures.

MAKE IT AS
BEAUTIFUL AS
YOU CAN

The handsome man said *do you want to make footprints?* His teeth were bright as a string of bulbs.

Sure, said Janet. *Sure.* Though, when he said *make footprints,* did he mean leave town or did he mean make love, or both? She never could understand things, really, but for this one, this handsome one, she'd go along.

Bring all your shoes. He flashed her a smile again.

Is that city talk? she asked. She pressed her forehead into his shoulder.

No, sweetheart, it's straight talk. Go home. Get all your shoes.

Janet came back with a carpetbag full of heeled oxfords and wellingtons and mary janes. He was propped against the slick black body of someone's Chrysler Coupé. He tossed her bag in the back and went in under the steering wheel and did some magic, and the car coughed awake, and the bright-lit path in front of it wheeled with snowflakes.

The road out of town was soft and quiet, and the dark huddled close around them. Janet's fingers tiptoed up the handsome man's thigh like a working girl's legs. He squeezed her hand like he was about to make an important declaration.

I've made footprints from here to Oklahoma to way out west, places you never heard of, he said. He leaned forward and squinted, fogging the windshield with his breath. *Always looking for just the perfect place to make footprints.*

I like making footprints, said Janet.

I know, he said. *I knew that about you moment I met you.*

Sometime later, maybe an hour, he cut the engine and Janet jerked awake, and the handsome man whispered, *here.*

Janet lay back and made to hike up her skirt, but he was already out the door, pulling her carpetbag off the seat. She followed him out to the edge of a wide open field. He tossed the carpetbag down and said *we'll divide 'em up.* Then he tore into the bag like a hog feeding on scraps, grabbing any old shoe to his chest. *Whatever gets you going,* said Janet. She grabbed up whatever she could hold. She followed the handsome man to the snow-swollen lip of the field, and he said, *I go this way, you go that way. Make it as beautiful as you can.*

And there he went, loping away like a heavy deer, pressing shoes into the snow in practiced patterns. Here a pump, here a flat brogue. He made a flower and an angel and a likeness of a horse that would have impressed any bird flying overhead.

Are you kidding? called Janet. But he was already halfway across the field. *Hey, when are we going to make footprints, if you know what I mean? Really make footprints?*

Snow fell all around. Snow brushed Janet's cheek like the back of a gentle hand.

DAGUERREOTYPES

1. Hidden Mother

A slight mother could be disguised as a swaddling blanket or a bassinet. A larger mother was an overstuffed chair, a settee, an imposing piece of furniture. Careless practitioners might toss a rug over the mother, barely cloaking her shape. Ill-disguised mothers looked like bodies smuggled in the night. But such mistakes were for amateurs. Sargent was an expert at hiding mothers.

For instance, once he was commissioned to photograph a child named Eustace: a consumptive whose eyes were ringed blue as plums and whose whoop rattled the windowpanes. The boy teetered on the edge of death like a drip fattening on the rim of a faucet.

It will be hard to photograph the boy, said Sargent to the mother, *for all his whooping.*

And the mother pressed her puffy gloved hands on the boy's shoulders and hugged him down to two-thirds his size, whereupon he let out a small satisfied wheeze. Sargent cloaked that mother in a bearskin, hands-in-paws, face shadowed by a jagged row of teeth. The tintype was a sickly boy in the clutches of a stiff bear rug.

Another dumpling-faced infant could not abide anything but steady and consistent patting on her rump. She howled when left alone. The answer, said Sargent: a christening gown, made giant enough for the mother. The baby's head just peeked above the frilly tent. In the tintype, she smiled.

And one child was deceased. Sargent asked the mother if she might not like to be in the photo with the limp child, unhidden. But she shook her head and swiped the last sheen away from her daughter's brow. That mother was the soft inside of the casket, draped in silk.

There was also the phenomenon of the mother remaining hidden well after the photograph had been snapped and developed and framed and set on a mantel. This happened often enough in Sargent's line of work. Children would grow into adolescence with the love and support of an ottoman or a few yards of muslin. Several mothers, once he'd cloaked them for a photograph, had confided in Sargent that the disguise might make their mothering easier. A child might never grow to resent the constant presence of a large throw pillow. Might never notice it at all.

Only once did Sargent receive a complaint. Years of success had allowed him to move into a grander studio with more natural light, and he ushered a parade of mothers and children through it daily. Late afternoon, the golden hour, a young man, seventeen or eighteen years old, entered the studio and flopped onto Sargent's couch. The boy was milk-pale, his eyes ringed a deep violet. He was pursued by a bear rug that sat beside him on the couch and crossed its legs politely at the ankles.

You must stop her! said the boy.

The bear gave him a piteous look.

Sargent considered the request. In retrospect, the bearskin had been a bold statement. But years had shrunk the skin to accommodate the mother, or the mother had grown to fit the skin. Sargent could not imagine how to peel it from her. Besides, he feared the teeth.

2. *Lace*

This was his earliest trick, but he never tired of repeating it: a cutting of lace on a contact print, left for some moments in the sun. Then the exposure was stopped, and the impression of the lace was there always, ghosting white against a burned-dark background. He made sure to perform this trick with every variation of lace he came across, to see how each might reproduce photographically. Inevitably, the lace came attached to women.

His first cutting was separated from the hem of a petticoat. He did not ask the petticoat-owner's permission; he was already underneath the petticoat and merely plucked a nimble pair of scissors from his breast pocket while he was busy at work on other matters. This lace was simple and cheap; sun poked through its holes with ease and made a clear impression on the contact paper. He found he tired of the impression immediately after making it. Even now, he cannot remember the name of its owner.

Then he collected society laces: soft, complex. Some came from Paris and some were hand-hewn by American dressmakers. Some from cuffs and some from bibs and some from pillowcases. Each carried its own scent—rosewater, ash—though this was beyond his ability to reproduce.

The thing about lace—the very thing—was that to photograph it in his signature way was also to make it, almost exact as the original, only with more efficiency. Where women with tired hands labored days or weeks, he harnessed the power of the sun—the pencil of nature, he called it—to draw it in minutes.

The widow's lace that came from his mother's veil made an even stronger impression. The black of it beat back the sun. When he removed it from the contact paper, its twin gleamed crisp and white like the wedding gown she kept in the trunk at the foot of her bed.

The pencil of nature! He sounded it out in big round vowels, like for a child or a pet. He pointed to his work. *The pencil of nature!* Beside him, his mother held the photograph he'd made and, with an old and jet-ringed finger, traced and retraced the impression of her widow's weeds.

LORD BYRON'S
TEEN LOVER,
CLAIRE CLAIRMONT

As he undid her maidenhead he also seemed to tie knots inside her by invisible thread, so that when he left the inn she felt a new tug—a strand that snaked between her legs and found anchor in her heart. It only increased with distance.

Good-bye! he said. He buttoned his vest, a burning candle mirrored in each gold button; a column of flames. *Do not write me again!*

That night, on loose sheets, she began her first and only work, *The Idiot*.

I am full of poetry, she thought. With one hand she worked the quill. The other tested a nipple he'd sucked, still wet.

She felt a tug toward Switzerland. This must be his direction. Easy enough to swing her party of poets from the Lake District to Lucerne: her sister, heavy with child, and her brother-in-law, with stormy brow and many loose sheets of poems Claire had made in fair copy for him. Homeless, all three.

They would rent a villa. They would commune with Byron. When they arrived, he was not yet there. They waited six full days, each working at a manuscript. Sometimes Claire watched her companions write, each lost somewhere inside themselves. Each leagues ahead of Claire. Sometimes, when she watched them, she was never so alone.

He arrived with peacocks and private physician. He arrived in a fortune teller's cart. He arrived with reddened lips, a smudge of kohl about his eyes.

And there was Claire, snuck into his villa by way of open window. Stretched on his soft-made bed, fanning herself with her thin manuscript. *I am a poet,* she said.

Go away, said Byron. He pressed a ticking muscle in his temple.

He communed with the other poets in her party. The men went out on the lake in a paddleboat: Byron and Shelley, small against the water. Claire watched from shore, heeded the tug toward him, increased *The Idiot.* Ten pages became twenty. Twenty became thirty. She watched Lord Byron at dinner, in his shirtsleeves, misting the air with wit. The way he encircled Mary Shelley's wrist with one browned hand. The way he avoided Claire's own gaze. That evening, by lamplight, *The Idiot* grew.

Mornings, she waited in the shadow below his balcony. As he composed above her, she felt the scratch of his quill as on her own pages. His physician took to eating cherries, launching the stones off the balcony in arcs. They landed with soft thumps.

Perhaps *The Idiot* was a novella. It kicked at her from where she was knotted. One afternoon, long after Byron had retreated into his villa and she was alone in the shade of his balcony, she wrote a single sentence that was more than itself. She read it aloud. The sentence was for her and for the whole world. She read it again. She returned to her own villa and the sentences came clear and glinting, like the waves that scalloped the lake. This was a new feeling. She could make her own world. She made more of it. Sometimes she worked all night and stumbled to breakfast with circles under her eyes. Sometimes, when she made words, she forgot her reason for making them at all. It was the words, only. And the words were enough.

But, by the pull of the thread in her, Claire felt *The Idiot* must pass before Byron's Adriatic eyes. Only he knew what work was good. And she thought *The Idiot* might be very good. When it reached one hundred pages, when she could no longer keep it hid, she sneaked into his villa through the same unlatched window. She found the door to his chamber. She knocked. There was no answer. She pressed her lips to the keyhole.

You must read The Idiot, she called.

Still no answer.

I need you!

She rattled the knob. She slapped her palms against the door. She called his name, again and again. She knocked until her knuckles ached.

She slumped against the door, manuscript in hand. And she slept, head cocked against the jamb.

She was half-awake when Byron lifted her upright. His eyes deep and distant. His breath heady with spirits. His curls all off to one side. The thread reeling taut, at last. She remembered her purpose.

Will you read The Idiot? she whispered.

Byron smiled. He traced the collar of her blouse, where it opened.

In her hand, the manuscript soft from clutching.

No, he said. *What nonsense.*

For a moment, she made to back away from his touch. For a moment, she clutched her work tighter. Then, his hands around her waist. Their expert pressure.

It squeezed the nonsense out of her, at once.

Her loosening grip. Her letting go. *The Idiot*'s pages strewn on the floor, where they would soon be trod upon, torn, crumpled, thrown away. Being near brilliance, she knew, demanded some loss. And some stories, like some infants, were too frail to meet the world.

The thread between them so short, and so fine.

TALKING DOLLS

Making Herself a Factory Machine
West Orange, New Jersey, October 1889

The foreman held a doll by the waist: open-mouthed china face revealing a row of surprising china teeth, blinking glass eyes that looked on everything.

The foreman was young. He had a carefully brushed amount of hair and a fresh mustache. He was in his shirtsleeves and his shirt was dimpled by the tightness of suspenders that clung to his lean shape. Shirtsleeves didn't seem right but Emily supposed it was vigorous, factory work: too vigorous for a jacket. He smiled back at the office he'd come from, as if someone there had made a joke. Then he turned the crank, and the doll, like some creature from another world, spoke—*Mamma, I love you oh so much, but, Mamma, I'm tired.* Emily felt a leap; she looked for the source of the sound. The mouth was still. The voice came from the chest, like the doll's own heart was crying for Mother. Never before had she heard a doll talk. Dolls were meant for secrets and whispered play. But here was the doll's noise. And the foreman spoke over it all: the doll, the grinding Ediphones, the girls who unfurled on both sides of Emily. A ribbon of girls from end-to-end of the factory, each reciting a nursery rhyme or singing a song.

There's a cylinder inside the doll. The foreman came close and turned the doll around and teased its clothes aside to show a lever that reset the needle inside her. *So, all these girls here are making recordings of their voices, to go on the cylinders.*

Can I try her? Emily reached out, palms-up, and the foreman laid the doll in her hands. Though she was nearly seventeen, she felt like a little girl, the way her spirit leapt at being given this small confidante. The foreman stood back and crossed his arms. He watched. Emily felt his stare bumping along the dull black buttons that climbed the black bodice that surrounded the corset that clutched her.

Heavy, said Emily. She rocked the doll.

Don't shake it. Delicate machinery in there.

When Emily turned the crank, the voice that came was not a voice but a demon call, tight and screeching. *MammaIloveyouohsomuchbutmammaI'mtired.*

You're turning it too quick, he said.

The foreman reset the doll and gave it back, and Emily tried the crank again. Again, the demon call.

Forget it. The foreman took the doll. Emily's hands fell to her lap, and for a moment there was the nervous ache of metal on her tongue and down the hatch of her throat. She needed this job, had woken so early and walked so many blocks to win it, had been awarded one of only a few places at the special Edison factory, and what if she'd ruined things already? What would Emily say to her aunt, who had found the job for her in the first place?

The foreman smiled as if she'd done some charming mischief.

He hovered over Emily and showed her how to do the work: fit a tin cylinder on the Ediphone, flick the machine into action, read a poem or song off a sheet of paper and into the horn. Her mouth had to be very close to the horn.

The foreman pouched his lips to the horn, to show how recording must be done. Lips kissing the horn, dispassionate and close. He spoke in a tight-snipped voice, his imitation of a factory girl: *What are little boys made of? Snips and snails and puppy dog tails, that's what little boys are made of!* His thick hands playing in the lamplight. Emily laughed.

His voice, forever a series of lines.

He offered the delicate cylinder. She took it, this band of time, tucked it into her pocket.

And this was the afternoon: hundreds of cylinders, each a doll's voice, each fitted into a body that would travel far beyond New Jersey. Emily's voice would fill nurseries across the country, in Europe, maybe even China. Places she'd never go. She imagined her voice called up, without her knowing, in fantastic rooms occupied by strange little girls who walked backwards and spoke in curled and loopy tongues. Sometimes she looked behind her, studied the rows of doll-constructors. Their careful use of tools. Their blank faces above those pale and ageless faces, the china faces they lifted and turned, painted, fitted with eyes, attached to tin bodies, tin voice boxes.

Too soon, doll voicing was only work. Emily divided it into a series of gestures: reach for the cylinder, fit it onto the machine, flick the switch, read off the paper, flick the switch, and—in one motion—arc the cylinder off the Ediphone and into the crate. Turn to the next page, the next rhyme. Some morsel of childhood typed out by machine. The room hummed on.

Living could be divided into such gestures. Dividing life into gestures—small, smaller—might make it just easy enough to continue living. This, she thought, was how her own mother and father had done life, when they'd lived. Here was the memory of them again, still and momentary as dolls. Emily took them up. They were sewn of soft cloth, their faces dashed on in bright, loose stitches: a red smile, blue Xs for eyes, loops of brown yarn for Mama's hair, Poppa's handsome nose an L. She dared to touch them together, made them kiss as they had done each day, mornings before Poppa left for work and evenings after the dishes had been washed and the smell of boiled dinner still lingered.

Soon she put these dolls away. She did so by dividing the gesture into ever-smaller gestures. By making herself a factory machine. By lifting her eyes to where her single electric lamp gave off some filmy light. By following, hopeful, the silhouette of the foreman, who drifted behind the row of girls, watching. By deciding, *No, I shall not play with dolls again.*

A figure curled into her stall. The neighbor to her right. A pouch-faced girl with fine, mousey hair pulled into a drooped bun.

Switch, she said.

The girl took Emily's sheaf of papers, traded them with her own.

The doll-voicers and doll-constructors had fifteen minutes' lunch. They sat outside in the October sun, legs tipped up on steps, or perched on barrels and pallets. They ate heels of bread and bits of cheese. Emily had no lunch, hadn't thought to bring one. Here were the doll-voicers, all sitting at a rough picnic table.

Scoot over, said the pouch-faced girl to the girls beside her, bumping them with an elbow.

The pouch-faced girl had a tin lunch pail. *Haven't you ever worked before?* she said. *You'll get hungry.* She reached into the pail, plucked out a bruised apple, and set it in front of Emily.

The pouch-faced girl was Sarah, and this was their friendship: Emily sat next to Sarah. She sat next to her in the factory, where they switched sheets, and she sat next to her at lunch, where Sarah told Emily about her sisters, all four of them, and how she cared for them all. In turn, Emily spoke of her Aunt's rules and how much she paid for room and board—almost everything she made. Nights, the two walked home side by side.

And the foreman. At the end of the day he dismissed them, each. One day, as the girls passed him, he laid his hand on Emily's shoulder. The warm weight of it. *Good evening.*

Good evening! said Sarah. She looped her hard arm through Emily's arm. And Emily was dragged out into the night air, marched through the yard, gravel skittering from her feet. Sarah walked with chin jutted forward, swinging her lunch pail as they hurried from the factory.

You don't know what happened to Clara Smith, so I might as well tell you. This was before you was ever here. Sarah didn't look at Emily while she said this, but at the flittering lights of Orange, both of them heading toward the neighborhood where they lived in corners of apartments rented by relatives who could not love them like their parents had.

The foreman was friendly with Clara, too. You know what I'm going to say next, don't you?

Emily did know.

They sent her away. A maternity hospital in Albany, some of the girls said.

Emily thought—guilty thought—there never was a Clara.

Over the months, Emily had grown to like Sarah. She liked her in spite of her sharpness and the hard-formed confidence she wore over what was surely loneliness. It seemed Sarah cared too much about the foreman. Her muttered reproaches and the hatefulness she cast at his back, his kind back.

He's no good, said Sarah, as if she read Emily's mind.

A Sweet, Hot Thing That Kicked Up, Now
Boston, Massachusetts, December 1889

The doll! Too heavy to be tucked into the branches of the Christmas tree, she rested beneath its shaggy limbs. In her eyes, a reflection of the fairy lights dangling from branches above, the flames that spat inside their glass bellies, and of the family that gathered, now, around the tree: Mother in new garnet earrings; straight-backed Father, straighter than the back of his oak chair; Grandmother Rose pinching a cross-stitched book-mark—a gift from her granddaughters, who had shared in the stitching, though you couldn't tell their stitches apart—between her yellowed fingernails. They watched in silence as the sisters lifted the long-anticipated doll away from her resting place. Her inner machinery heavy enough that both sisters had to clutch her.

Her eyes were sleeping eyes: lashes that batted her china cheeks. Her chest tocked in a curious way when she was hoisted. Dangling at her wrist, a tag: THOMAS EDISON'S FAMOUS TALKING DOLL.

And here were the sisters, in matching new-made pinafores, white lace for Christmas, knotted snug at their backs by their rough-handed nurse. Their tumbling pigtails and rumpled stockings. These sisters were at precisely that point when a little girl is an even more perfect shape and size than her doll. And each was a copy of the other: a single birthmark twinned their upper lips; a sideward glance seemed to skate across the face of one sister and onto the face of the other. Now they held the doll between them and searched for the crank. When they found it, both took hold.

Here was the noise: shrieking metal, the spirit of an angry child scrabbled up from the grave. Mother recoiled; Father furrowed his brow; Grandmother Rose waved a knotty hand before her face as if she might shoo the child-banshee away.

And the twins, to their relatives' surprise, swatted each other's hands.

You turned it too quickly!

No, you snatched at it!

I didn't!

Reluctant Mother, calling for Nurse. Nurse, still chewing breakfast, hurrying from somewhere deep within the house to separate the girls, to place the doll in the hands of one and then the other. As each took her turn with the crank, the other glared at her sister, willing the demon voice to return. And it did; neither girl could call up a girl voice from the toy. One sister sat on the rug, dumb as a doll, and cried while the other pressed her fists into her own eye sockets to make colors bloom behind her lids. All this observed by the grown relatives, who clutched the arms of their chairs.

Now, the doll was passed among the grownups. First, Nurse, who cooed that Dolly only needed some care and patience. She cranked with three ruddy fingers pinched around the handle, pinkie raised like to whisper *careful, careful.* The girls gathered close, watching. One hung her head on Nurse's shoulder. One leaned, eager, on the heels of her hands. And still, the shriek. Nurse's face, a brief twist into some adult disappointment. A look that betrayed her life beyond the nursery, the house: that suggested she'd seen a thing or two she didn't like, before.

Give it to Mother. Here was Mother's hand, outstretched and shivering, that seldom lifted anything heavier than a handkerchief. Nurse hoisted the doll into Mother's dipping arm, and Mother quick lurched forward to catch the heavy toy, lifting it roughly in a way the girls had never seen. She sat the doll on her lap, where the sisters had never sat. With one finger, she brushed back its bouncy curls: such alien tenderness her daughters watched in silence. The translucence of her fingernail just as it caught the light. The doll's curls, snagging like ribbon. Even this: the look she wore, a young girl's look. A curious tangle, like one who would give everything to be a girl again, to sit on the rug with her own doll.

She turned the crank.

The demon call.

And Mother's fallen face, the small slump that registered only in the loosening of the crepe about her shoulder blades, the way her grip sagged around the doll's waist, the toy tilting in her lap. A tremendous failure.

Mother, she said, her gaze fixed somewhere on the rug, *would you like to try the doll?*

Keep it away, said Grandmother Rose.

It's broken, Kitty. Here was Father, her husband. *Broken machinery.*

He reached for it. The doll, in Father's serious hands: another vision for his daughters. Father touched pens and inkwells. Father touched long guns and dead ducks with floppy necks and the flag that wagged on the pole in the yard, that he alone raised and lowered daily. Had Father ever touched a doll, before? The action of his fingers as he reset the needle. The fold of his brow above his troubled eyes. Maybe the final gesture ever shared between these sisters: a look, a weird bob in the chest that said isn't it strange to see Father puzzling over this poor frilly creature? To see him sheepishly pull aside the dress where it's slit and clutch the cool tin body in his reluctant hands, the doll's audacious yellow curls drooping onto his knees?

Twinkletwinklelittlestarrhowiwonderwhatyouarrrr!

Father, scrutinizing the doll. Staring into the china face, the glass eyes. The sleeping lids that were slow to open to him.

Defective, he said to the doll.

One sister, hoisting herself off the rug, going to stand by Father. The other, preoccupied now by her own new coral bracelet, a gift from Grandmother Rose that she turned around and around on her small brown wrist.

She'll have to go back, said Father.

Oh.

Here was the twin who stood by Father. Now a deep sadness set in, sympathy for this doll who must be shut up in a box, banished from this parlor, this family, this city, and lugged by careless postmen back to the terrible lonely place she was made, where she'd maybe be destroyed. The sister pictured a man with a hammer, smashing her china face to powder.

But she's still nice, isn't she? Look at her dress, she tried. *It's very fine.*

We'll buy you a fine dress like hers. No use keeping a broken doll just for her dress.

I've sewn nicer dresses than that for your old dollies, said Grandmother Rose. *Oh, stop now with the crying, young lady. How spoiled you are. Look how nicely your sister sits!*

Sister on the rug, still turning the bracelet round her wrist. In this sister, a sweet hot thing that kicked up, now, and kicked harder as Father explained how wronged she'd been, how wronged all of them had been, how expensive this item and how difficult to acquire, what a sham they'd fallen for, what an unconscionable scoundrel Thomas Edison, who cared only about profits and not about little girls. *He hates little girls, is what it is,* said Father.

The sharp-edged word *hate* twirled in her mind, a keen little gemstone. Did she *hate?* Who could she *hate?* Thomas Edison, yes. All the Edison people who'd ruined her present. She saw them, Hecates, twisting and battering the insides of the doll before tossing them in like rubbish. Or maybe they'd sabotaged only one small part: a tooth on a gear, bent by an intentional finger, while they'd laughed. She *hated* them.

She had more hate. She swirled her gaze around the room, everyone caught in it: Mother, lips pursed and hand rested on Father's fist; Grandmother Rose, stroking the tassel that hung from her new bookmark; Nurse and the knot of brown bread still in her hand from breakfast; her sister, watery-eyed, pleading with Father; Father and his stiff grasp on the doll—the doll! She leveled her hate onto it. The doll took her hate, pulled it into her joints and her useless tin body and her sweet dumb face. The doll took so much hate she was surprised it didn't crack apart. Father handed it to Nurse, who would carry it, soaked with hate, and pack it back into its box, and return it full of hate to the horrible place it had come from.

Contents of the Desk of William H. Meadowcroft, personal secretary to Thomas Edison
West Orange, NJ, catalogued 1967 by National Park Service

- TELEPHONE on extension arm
- DESK LAMP with glass shade
- MEMO BOOKS, 3
- DESK BASKETS, 3
- MIMEOGRAPH SILKS, STACKED
- CARBON PAPER, STACKED
- LETTER PAPER with letterhead
- PAY ENVELOPES, 3
- INKSTAND
- PAPER FASTENER, common 20th century office supply
- McGill's STAPLES #1
- BLUE PENCILS, 2

- CEDAR PENCILS, 5
- RUBBER ERASER, Velvet brand
- RUBBER STAMP HOLDER, common early 20th century
  office supply
- RUBBER STAMPS, 5
- STAMPING INK, bottle
- FOUNTAIN PENS, 3
- TIMESHEETS, 20
- DESK CALENDAR
- BOOKS, various
- FILES, various
- SCISSORS
- DESK BLOTTER
- TINTYPE PHOTOGRAPH of wife, Phoebe, and sons
  William and Charles
- TOOTHBRUSH, common early 20th century celluloid
  toiletry
- TOOTH POWDER TIN, Eucryl brand
- CORRESPONDENCE, various
- TRAIN SCHEDULES, New York Central & Hudson River
  Railroad, Central Railroad of New Jersey, New Jersey
  and New York Railway, Morris & Essex Railroad
- GOLD RING, early 20th century, possibly wedding band
- CYLINDER, tagged "Tin Phonograph Cylinder [. . .]
  Record"—bent, unplayable

The Predictable Ups and Downs of a Waveform
Silicon Valley, September 2014

The cylinder arrived at the lab carefully packed in layers of tissue and foam. This, thought Carl, was the hallmark of a librarian: the careful packing. His wife, Marjorie, was a librarian, and she kept her own museum in the spare room, full of family photos organized into a card catalogue, swatches of 1970s French fabric from his parents' old tailoring shop preserved in plastic sleeves and clicked into a 3-ring binder, and childhood things—his, hers, their grown children's—swathed in the same tissue as the ring. Some acid-free tissue, ordered online, that came on a comically big roll.

Librarians had spoken to Carl first. A breathy conference call he'd taken too early on a Monday. The librarians were well into their coffees by then, New Jersey time ahead of his Californian, and the coffees had brought out their accents, and their accents yawned around what they had to say.

So, Dr. Hilling? We have a little phonograph record. It's in terrible shape. Hello, Dr. Hilling? Is this working?

Carl scratched a spot of grime off the table where he sat. *I'm here.*

I can't get used to this new thing. We just replaced it. Well, this piece has been in our collection for a long time. It's a little banged up. We think . . . yes, we think this is a doll voice. It might be a woman's voice on there. It sat in the bottom of a drawer for eighty years before we found it.

Another librarian chimed in. *It's a tough old cylinder.* A joke. Carl forced out a laugh. Very little was funny to him, he'd discovered. Maybe it was his programmer's logic. He sniffed.

So here was the cylinder: solid tin, small as a child's bracelet, time-battered into more of a star shape than a circle. A ratty tag dangled from a meager length of string. The tag was written out in the sort of inky hand that had died with the advent of ballpoint. *Tin phonograph cylinder & record.* Carl liked the double lines beneath the handwriting: a firm mattress for the words to rest on. Nonetheless, he patiently removed the tag, taking time to unknot the labeler's knots. Victorian knots, either loose enough to make you wonder how they survived the years, or pulled so tight the strands blended, over time, into a fibrous button. The knots came undone and Carl set the tag aside.

Carl did the cylinder the way Carl did every recording: slid onto a plastic mandrel arm he had made, himself, after careful measurements. The cylinder turned and turned as the scanner's eye did its work, creeping dots of red and white pinpricking the grooves. Carl watched the image grow on his monitor: a series of open tunnels, careful-cut and square. The rare chisel groove, pre-1899. A yawp of excitement. He wanted to turn to a colleague and say, *look at this chisel groove!* But there was no one else.

Carl pointed to the screen. *Chisel groove,* he said to Robert, who was just arriving now, already wearing the slippers he wore every day at the lab. Robert held a blue mug, slanted to one side like it had been stretched, that said, *Linux: I did it my way.* He watched the slanty mug each time he brought it to his mouth, matching his lips with its slanty rim.

Looking good, said Robert. He said little else, and for a long time the two watched the grooves. When the scan was finished, Robert took Carl's seat and called up some software and some difficult lines of code, and Carl watched Robert analyze the grooves, lay a computerized mesh over the grooves, extract from the grooves a single waveform that sketched itself across the screen.

All the while, Carl tried to cast himself back to sometime before 1899. Anything before 1900, in his mind, was like a print by Currier and Ives: children in curly-bladed skates frolicking on frozen ponds, horses whose legs seemed forever arrested mid-trot, steamboats sending up flags of smoke over the Mississippi. Even the photos from that century were, somehow, unreal. It was difficult to care about these figures who stared out from the daguerreotypes his wife collected, their stiff eyes and hard folded hands, the stands that stilled them for the photo just visible behind their patent leather feet. Harder, still, to feel anything for blurred figures on porches, faceless boys on bicycles, men and women at work in butcher shops and dry goods stores, or even dead soldiers on the battlefield.

Old technology, thought Carl, was the culprit. The scratchy record, the telegraph message, the tintype—anything we don't know how to use anymore—was a barrier to feeling. Modern technology made him feel something. Scan and colorize a Civil War photo and, suddenly, here is a boy—full of breath and blood, as real as a neighbor or a person on the street—too small for his Union coat.

The work was done. Robert forced out a sharp sigh. Carl had forgotten Robert, who ran two hands over his bald scalp. Long work, this. Repetitive work, laying a mesh over an old recording, digitizing the grooves, the predictable up-downs of a waveform. They did two or three recordings a day, this way.

I need another coffee, said Robert. He pressed play.

The voice of a girl. Carl didn't expect the strange way she talked: as if someone had sat her down and told her: think of a doll. Now make that doll's voice. *A horse has four legs!* she warbled. Between phrases, the hiss of the groove. *One on each corner!* The recording ended. Robert played the recording again.

A horse has four legs!

He played it over and over, calling her voice back from the century before, scrubbing the noise, playing it again until the whine came almost clear. Robert played and replayed, and Carl thought of everything he knew about Edison's factory. He'd seen photos of proud men with handlebar mustaches. The women he'd seen in the photos never had names, but held some equipment or looked bashfully at the floor.

Kind of annoying, isn't she? Robert asked the screen.

But Carl couldn't stop listening to the voice, that strange warble out of time. After Robert left, he played it again, and here was the same woman made alive in a nursery rhyme. At the end of the recording, she died. There was something different about this recording, different from all the others he'd scanned. The distant doll-voice. Here was the voice of a young woman on the edge of something—he didn't know what.

Carl pressed play. Time wound back; the woman lived. She died.

Much Lighter Now
West Orange, New Jersey, January 1890

This was the last thing Emily ever read into the Ediphone: *A horse has four legs, one on each corner.* She paused a moment after reading it, and read it again to herself. Was it funny? She imagined herself holding a doll who said this to her. It seemed a sassy thing for a doll to say.

After that, she switched off the Ediphone and switched off her electric reading lamp and joined the line of girls that spooled from the factory into the cool dark of the evening. She'd grown used to arriving at work in the dark and leaving in the dark and only seeing light filtered through the factory's high-slung windows. Sarah was beside her in line. Behind them, the doll-constructors who spent days careful-placing the doll machinery in the doll bodies, testing the dolls and fluffing their wigs and painting their features. Now they muttered about their children and their husbands and wives, who waited for them at home.

Next day, when Emily arrived, there were no Ediphones, no electric lamps, no sheaves of paper, no desks. There were heaps and heaps of dolls. There was the foreman and there was another

Edison fellow in tweed who stood beside a crate filled to the top with doll machinery. Another crate was full of cylinders.

The foreman held a naked doll. All the workers filtered in around him. Tired faces of doll-assemblers mixed with the tired faces of doll-voicers: girls whose futures already showed.

Ladies and gentlemen, said the foreman. This was strange.

Instructions from Mr. Edison. Until we're through every doll, everyone will be doing this. He laid the doll on a worktable and the crowd leaned in. With a screwdriver, he opened her body. Inside was her machine: the tiny speaker, the cylinder, the careful gears that turned it. He pried it all out, using the long point of the screwdriver for leverage. Separated cylinder from machine and tossed each into a crate. Then he closed the hollowed doll, screwing her empty tin body up tight. He weighed her in his hand. *Much lighter, now,* he joked. Leaning in, Emily saw Sarah glare, full faced, at him. For the first time, his eyebrows leapt at Sarah's disapproval.

A stream of questions for the foreman. *Why are we doing this,* and *how long are we doing this,* and *what will happen to the machines?* One girl added: *and to the dolls?* And the answers: the dolls are a disaster. All returns. The machines will be broken down for parts. The doll bodies will be sold without voices. The cylinders will be melted down, remade into other tin things.

A ripple among the girls. A ripple, Emily imagined, that sounded like all their voices melted together.

And our jobs? asked a worker, a middle-aged woman who'd been tasked with dressing the dolls in gowns and hats and snuggling them into boxes. There was a long silence.

You are welcome to apply for jobs at any of the other Edison factories, said the Edison fellow. The foreman looked at him like a little boy looks at his teacher. Emily knew this was his boss.

You young ladies doing voices, said the Edison fellow, *are the very first ladies ever recorded on an Edison cylinder.* A doll-voicer cleared her throat.

Opening the dolls, removing their insides. Emily did this for the next several days. She worked beside a man she knew only in passing; he had built the cranks for the dolls' machines.

Even the foreman did this work. Sometimes Emily watched him from down the line. He worked slow, teasing out the hours, setting the pace for everyone else. Only Sarah sped ahead, working out some anger on the dolls, dislodging their tin guts with single stabs. Nights, on their walks home, Emily asked no questions.

And then the work was done. Someone screwed together the final body of the final doll, and the defunct workers stepped out from behind their tables and squinted. It was morning on a Wednesday. They hadn't even got in a full day of work. They would have to return home, now, with whatever pay they were owed, or head out straight away for another factory where they might find a job. Even this disappointment didn't stop them from lining up, as they always did, on their way out. The foreman, grave now, thanked each person as they left for the last time. When he went to thank Sarah, she shouldered away from him and out the door.

Emily was last. And here was the young foreman. *I'm going to work in the lamp factory,* he said. What was she expected to say to this?

My aunt takes in washing sometimes, she offered. *I helped her before.*

Emily. It was Sarah. She waited outside the door, clutching herself tight around the waist, impatient, and jiggling her lunch pail with the other hand.

Can I walk with you? asked the foreman. Emily looked for a moment at Sarah, who already knew the ending to this story.

Emily let the foreman take her arm, let him lead her from the factory and lock its door behind them. There was Sarah, already rushing away toward their neighborhood. Emily might never again see Sarah, who could go to another factory or another city or another state, for all she knew. But she thought of their voices, blended with those of the other girls into a chorus, and found comfort in the vision. None would ever lose the others. None would suffer the violence of play that ruined dolls and left them lonely when girls grew up. And none would be taken against their wills to places they had no desire to go: strange rooms, strange darknesses.

Then the quiet of time.

A COLLECTOR

On their sixth date he led her into his soft-carpeted bedroom, made amber by sconces, past his bachelor's bed and his night table grayed on top with a fine layer of dust and past the tamped-down cat pad in the corner, to an arts-and-crafts dresser with many brass-handled drawers.

Started collecting these in 1970, he said. He worked open a drawer.

Inside were eggs, in dappled blues and greens and some in salmon pinks and splotches of brown.

Agnes recoiled. The dullness of them, fossilized and un-changing, nested into these tea towel-lined drawers: there was horror in the vision. It wormed into her gut. To gain her composure she reached out for something and took hold of her date's shoulder, which was hard, crisper than his new button-down shirt, still creased by the package's cardboard insert.

He stiffened. Then, lifted a long hand onto Agnes's hand, patted where it was plumpest. Momentarily he turned around and smiled at Agnes. She observed, then, that his head was the dome-shape and grizzled-pink color of a buzzard's, though she had never seen the top of a buzzard's head. In fact, she'd never seen a buzzard. But she knew what one looked like.

He worked open a lower, larger drawer, revealing larger eggs.

Ostrich, he said. *Bald eagle. Some quite rare.* He lifted a beautiful egg out of the bottom-most drawer. An opalescent egg. Nature's loveliest commingling of green and darker green, of loamy browns and Mediterranean blues. *Avocet*, he said. *My rarest. These've all died out.* And he took Agnes's hand from his shoulder and turned it over, and he placed the egg in her palm.

Agnes turned the egg. The shell was cool, bumpy in places. The egg's elderly smell was cedar and mothballs and fusty sweetness.

And it struck Agnes all at once that she had just been handed a shelled corpse, a bird curled and fossilized, by this nice man who was now standing beside her, closing in for a kiss, lips already a white 'O,' eyes half-lidded like he was drifting into the sleep of old age.

The egg got heavy. It toppled off the tips of Agnes's fingers and thumped the carpet and rolled underneath the dresser. Agnes waited, worried for the sound of breakage. But there was no crack: only silence.

The old bachelor gasped, forgot the kiss. He got right down on his belly. He went after the egg, cheek pressed against the carpet, one arm patting blindly the space between the dresser and the floor.

ARE YOU
RUNNING AWAY?

Val says, *fuck school*. She eats another cracker. *Wouldn't it be great if school were canceled?* And I say yeah, it would be great. And she says, *I know a way*. She scrapes her shoed feet along her parents' couch. And I say, *How?* And she says, *There are these pipes*.

She shoves everything aside. Goldenrod, green, purple study notes. Her chem binder clicks open and the sheets slide everywhere, across the Persian rug and the hardwood and into corners of the room and up against Rolph the snoring yellow lab. She steps on the notes, leaves her dirty shoeprints on them. She doesn't care. I love Val because she doesn't care. The first time we met, in the change room before gym, she looked me up and down and said, *those boobs are low*. I could have hated her for that, but instead I was like, who says that? And I said, *thanks!* And, from then on, we were friends, even when everyone else pushed her away. Even when they asked *Her? Why?* and made sour faces. Later, we snuck things from the pockets of the backpacks students latched onto lockers when they went to gym: silver bracelets, digital watches, lip gloss. And after that, we started taking things from other places. If we wore our uniforms they'd let us into the best stores. In one walk around Club Monaco, Val lifted a sweater and three necklaces. Next time we went, shopping for dresses for the spring formal, we wore the necklaces at the checkout. And at Holt Renfrew, where every sales lady knew Val from dressing her mom, I took the key chains off every Moschino bag while Val twirled in a Marc Jacobs dress, all the salesladies cooing at her.

Later, I lined the key chains up on my bed. My mom came in right then, looking for her tennis shoes. My tongue tasted coppery.

Did you take them?

Why would I take your smelly runners?

I don't know why you do what you do.

It was too late to cover the key chains up; I just sat there, frozen, in front of my loot. She went straight for my closet and tossed my shoes around. She came over and lifted the skirt on my bed, stuck her whole head underneath. She tossed my pile of clothes off my desk chair. Then, she left. A few minutes later, I heard the front door slam, the car backing out of the driveway.

∽

Val already has the tools all packed up to do it. She's got this huge wrench. She slides it halfway out of the backpack waiting in her front hall, under the coat hooks, beside a line of about a hundred shoes, all her mother's. At the end of the row, her dad's runners.

Where the hell did you get that? I ask. And Val just laughs.

And then we're in front of school. The sun's going down, and we've just got sweatshirts over our blouses and ties, and we're still in our kilts and knee socks, and we're shivering. There are only a few cars left in the lot. A couple office lights are on. The windows of the Performing Arts Centre are cranked open, and we can hear singing.

They're right here, says Val. She pushes back some bushes against the wrought iron fence and there's a bunch of pipes snaking out and into the ground. *Give me the wrench.*

How did you find these? I ask. *I mean, were you, like, looking for them?*

She doesn't say anything. She just puts out her hand, twiddles her fingers.

In her backpack there's also clothes, a bag of chips, a makeup kit, a wallet, and a heavy Leatherman with a bunch of blades. The wrench is wrapped in a tie-dye tee shirt, worn-out and holey in places. Camp Wapomeo, 1998. The streetlamps and porch lights around us are dim, but when I unwrap the T-shirt, I can see the wrench handle's labeled in permanent marker: HAWTHORNE HALL.

∞

She calls her students idiots: this is her term of endearment. Some softer teachers call theirs kiddos or darlings. *Kiddo* and *darling* taste wrong, like a bad after-dinner mint. *Idiot* has a nice crisp mouthfeel and clear trajectory when she fires it off from the front of the room. And the girls love it, have always loved being called *idiots.* No matter what a girl says, what she loves most is a good strict teacher.

Like today, a girl fumbled something under her desk, and Ms. Wilson went around to where this student was fumbling and saw a pack of Camels. The girl was unwrapping the cello-phane in the shelf beneath the desk. For a whole minute she stood behind this girl and watched her. There was quiet in the room and the girl concentrated only on the wrapper, picking at it with her nails. The lecture on Yeats had stopped, and now all the other girls watched her watching their classmate, arms crossed, and their laughter started up. Finally, she rolled up the sheaf of handouts she held and bopped the girl on the head.

Idiot! she said.

Ow! said the girl. She pantomimed hurt, but she was laughing along with all the others.

You think I'm joking, she said, *but I'm not joking. You truly are an idiot. Give them to me.*

And the girl handed over the pack.

Do you want to be old before your time, hacking pieces of lung into a soggy tissue? Do you want to wheel your own oxygen tank around?

The girl giggled.

Don't laugh. Don't you dare laugh. You think I'm exaggerating? I've seen this with my own eyes. I lost someone very close to me this way. Very close to me.

The girl quieted but kept laughing under the quiet, shaking. All the other students laughed on, maybe now at the girl who wouldn't stop laughing even at this, and she had the sudden urge to slap this girl right across her laughing mouth. She lifted her tube of handouts and the girl mock cowered.

After the bell rang, the girl came up to her desk. Her blouse was unbuttoned at the collar and her tie was loose. Her blazer looked like it had been stuffed into the bottom of a locker for weeks. But she wore Chloé sunglasses on top of her head, and they were scratchless.

Ms. Wilson, said the girl. *Can I have my cigarettes back now?* She smiled a little.

Are you kidding me?

The girl looked around. *No. They're my property.*

Get out, she said. *Get out.*

Now she rests one hand on her pile of ungraded papers and one on the pack of Camels, like she's weighing one against the other. The night windows are mirrors, and in every pane a reflection of herself. Her small self. Her hooded eyes and downturned mouth. She has a sense that the girl with the cigarettes knew all along she was lying: that in fifty-five years she's never lost any of the few who are close to her, not even her grandparents.

∽

At the beginning of the semester, Val and I had stood in front of the wide mirror in the second-floor bathroom and tested out the word *cunts*. We started quiet, facing the mirror, looking at our mouths shaping out the word. The delicate C, the ear of a teacup. Then *unts*, like some character from *Lord of the Rings*.

Cunts, I said. All prim, like I was at a tea party. Like another way of saying thank you.

Val smiled. Her smile was silver. When she said it—*CUNTS!*— it was a sharp little bullet.

Cuuunts, I said.

CUNTS! she spewed.

Cunts? I said. *C-unts? Cunties!* I laughed. Val didn't laugh with me.

CUNTS! she returned. She was looking at herself in the mirror, glaring now. Her eyes were far away. *CUNTS! CUNTS! CUNTS! CUNTS! MOTHERFUCKING CUNTS!*

Right then, Mrs. Wylie came in and went into a stall. Val looked at me, not just in a wild way but in this way that said, *I'm going to fuck with you.* These sort of slitty eyes.

GODDAMN MOTHERFUCKING PIECE OF SHIT CUNT.

There was a voice from the stall. *Excuse me?*

Val was laughing now. *Cunt,* she'd said. Not *cunts.* Mrs. Wylie came wheeling out of the stall and up behind us wearing the angriest face I'd ever seen, and Val was still laughing even when Mrs. Wylie clamped a hand on her shoulder and spun her away to the principal's office. I saw her later that afternoon, after class, and she wouldn't tell me anything about the meeting.

☙

We are the chorus in *The Mikado.* Today we wear our kimonos for the first time, and everything looks like an old candy box, and we're about to do our first full dress rehearsal. Ms. Freund films us from a seat in the audience, taking notes. Ellen, our choreographer, watches too, gesturing along to the music. And Mr. Wimple, the orchestra conductor, lifts his thin arms for the first swell.

There's a step and a note that's impossible to reach. A small pirouette and a screeching high C. Even before costumes, this was a dizzying combination. We clattered against each other like bowling pins. Now we have to do it in sandals, holding and snapping fans. There are whispers in the wings. Some chorus girls pinch other chorus girls and some rest their anxious heads on others' anxious shoulders. We'll never make it.

☙

There's a nozzle on the end of one of the pipes, and Val cranks the wrench open to fit its jaws around this nozzle. But before she opens it, she puts the wrench down and turns to look at me. She's smiling. Her teeth glow green. The elastics on her braces are glow-in-the-dark. I've never noticed before.

I've got this idea, she says. *Let's lock the doors.*

I think about this for a minute. *But they're already locked.*

No, she says. *From the outside.*

She rummages in her backpack and comes out with the Leatherman. Scans it until she finds the screwdriver. I can hear my own blood. Sometimes this happens, when I worry.

What'll that do, though? I ask.

Are you stupid? It'll unscrew things.

She's already walking onto campus and I'm tripping along behind her. *No, I mean, why would we want to do that?*

Val doesn't answer. We're at the emergency exit beside the gym and she's unscrewing the handles on the doors. The first one falls off and clanks against the asphalt.

Val. I tug her hood. She's putting all her weight into unscrewing the other knob and her body's humming with anger, and so tense, like she's become hard metal. *Val.*

The second knob falls, and Val's headed for the door to the Science Wing.

Val. She pulls her hood up over her head, tucks her hands into her sleeves, looks around to make sure no one's watching.

Val! I grab her arm, but she snatches it away, and I think she's going to hit me or wrestle me to the ground the way she comes at me, with such force. But she grabs me into the biggest hug. She strokes my hair and kisses my forehead. And her mouth's a little slobbery because of her braces. She leaves a ring of spit I don't wipe off. For a minute we're just in a hug, really warm. I don't know if I've been this close to someone for a long time, since I was little. To feel their breathing and breathe against it. I could stay for a while. Val takes my hand and twists her fingers in mine. We walk hand-in-hand to every fire escape and do the work together.

⁂

She has also confiscated a lighter. She considers it now, in her hand. Cheap. Blue. Plastic. She flicks it into flame and imagines setting all her unfinished grading on fire, right now. Just throwing it in the waste bin.

Here are the other things she's confiscated: a silver Tiffany bracelet. A mohair sweater. A gift certificate for Victoria's Secret. A palm-sized leather Dachshund with beady black eyes. A tube of YSL lipstick. A laser pointer, which she used to make dots on her students' foreheads until she accidentally caught a girl in the eye.

Most girls don't ask for their things back. She wore the Tiffany bracelet once, on a trip to Montreal. No one noticed it was engraved with the wrong initials.

Sometimes she wonders what the girls care about. She's seen them take one glance at their grades and stuff their essays into the bottoms of their backpacks, not looking at the comments. Sometimes she finds them crumpled in the garbage. Sometimes soaked with pop or coffee.

She has never smoked a cigarette. She considers this too. Even in her youth, she always made the right decisions.

∽

Back at the nozzle, Val's not strong enough to twist it herself. We both grip the wrench and brace a leg against the pipe. The first twist is the hardest. When the nozzle budges, we fall and the wrench slips and thumps against the dirt. From there, all it takes is some unscrewing.

I guess I knew it but I didn't really know, or didn't want to: that we weren't hacking open some water main or steam pipe from the heating system.

Shit, I say. *Did you know this was gas? Val?*

Val's sitting back on her hands. She looks straight ahead, not even at the pipe but at something in her head, and her breathing's thick and even, and I've never been more alone. I pick up the nozzle and try to fit it back on, but it's heavy and my hands are useless and I can't get it straight. The smell of gas in my nostrils, in my lungs, everywhere.

Val grabs my hand and tugs me up to my feet. *Look,* she whispers.

Someone's at the window, up on the second floor where the English rooms are. A silhouette and light behind it.

And now we're running, running down the block, and I look back and think maybe I should yell something. Maybe I should yell, *gas leak!* Do people do that? Would anyone even hear? But Val's got me by the hand and there's no time to yell, we're too far away. We cut through Rosedale Park. And when we're halfway across the park, this huge dog comes at us out of nowhere, leash dragging behind. I'm ready to keep running, away from this dog that looks like a Shepherd and seems headed straight for us, but Val stops and crosses her arms, and when the dog sees this he stops, too. He circles. He watches Val for what she's going to do. He licks his long snout.

Val starts howling. Barking and howling, with her neck craned up and her face to the sky. And the dog starts howling, talking to her, and they exchange howls in some weird call and response. I stand there watching them howl at each other, and then Val stops, sudden.

Bad dog! She yells. *Bad! You're a bad dog!*

The dog cocks its head like it needs an explanation. Its owner's coming toward us now, from the other side of the park. I guess I'm cold, because I'm shivering like crazy, my teeth clattering. I back away with my arms across my chest.

Bad, bad dog!

There's a whistle, and the dog's ears perk up. It runs back the way it came, the tags on its collar jingling, and I'm left alone with Val.

∽

It's good the auditorium seats are mostly empty, because this is what happens during the pirouette: one of us kicks her sandal off. It flips off her rotating foot like the launch of a discus and just misses Ellen and Ms. Freund. Moments later, the clap of wood sandal against wall, somewhere we can't see. Some of us burst into laughs, but soon a sense of relief melts through us all. That was it. A flying sandal. A sudden slap.

We follow behind. We bow and shuffle. When we twirl, we're just colors. When we look up, the stage lights smudge in our eyes. When we lift our voices, they braid together and rise, and rise, and rise.

∽

Val and I are alone in the park now. She strips down and tosses her uniform onto the grass. For a second she stands there in her underwear, like a stopped animal just before it runs. Her ribs are so sharp you could climb them, and she's sick-pale, almost purple. Then she pulls layers from her bag: leggings and jeans and a tank top and tee shirt and sweatshirt and jacket. When she's dressed, she's just a person-shape. She pulls her hood up tight around her head. She hoists the backpack.

Go home, she says.

Where are you going? I ask.

Like you give a fuck.

What do you mean? I give a fuck.

Val's scanning the grass like she's lost something. She talks to the grass when she tells me this: *You just use me. You come over and eat my parents' food*—her parents, who she calls Thing 1 and Thing 2. Who she steals crunchy twenty-dollar bills from all the time—*and follow me around and, like, get your cheap thrills. You just want to see what it feels like to have everyone hate you. You don't. Give. A. Fuck.* She bends to pick up the Leatherman, glinting like her smile where it dropped.

You're wrong! It bursts out so hard, from some place in my gut. *And everyone doesn't hate you.* After I say it, I'm not sure. *Tell me where you're going,* I whisper. *Are you running away?*

Go get back on the honor roll, nerd. Val turns to leave. The shush of her feet on the grass. I pick up the pieces of her uniform and bundle them in my arms. She knows I'm there behind her, her shadow, but she doesn't turn around. I follow her to the end of the park, where it dumps out onto Highland Avenue and dead leaves skritch down the street. She steps into a splash of lamplight. And when I see her there, lit from the top and all skinny and mean, her long mean legs and her pinched-tight fists, something sick comes up from my stomach and punches its way out my mouth.

Why are you such a goddamn bitch?

It wasn't what I was going to say. I was going to say something that would make her come back. She doesn't even stop. She laughs, this tight bark. She walks off.

And I drop everything, and sit on the cold grass. The cold climbs up me, right through my guts and out the top of my head and on into space. *I just want to see what it feels like to have everyone hate me.* And I guess, in this moment, I know what it's like to be all alone, completely alone in the universe, with no love and no friends and no home. Val was my last and only friend in the world. And her face, when she said *get back on the honor roll, nerd*: this emptiness, like she never even really knew who I was.

The pipe. I think of it now the way you realize you've forgotten your history binder in your locker and you have a test tomorrow. It's still there, vomiting gas into the atmosphere. Probably the whole school's in a cloud of gas by this time. The memory speeds at me, brings this new sickness.

Before I hung with Val, I was friends with Stephanie Yip. We're not friends anymore, but—we used to go to her dad's electronics store and rake our fingers through the bins of chips and fuses and switches, braid friendship bracelets out of multi-colored wire. It felt so good, swimming my fingers through the tiny pieces, like nothing in the world mattered. I don't know why I think of this now, when I should be thinking of how to fix what we've done, whether to tell someone and who to tell and how much I'll get in trouble, but I'm there, raking my fingers through the pieces, and her dad is standing in the doorway cradling the phone against his cheek, speaking in Cantonese. If Stephanie ever hacked open a gas pipe, she'd just call her dad and he'd fix it. Once, she told me her dad kept twenty thousand dollars cash somewhere in the house, just in case.

∽

Comes a train of little ladies from scholastic trammels free, each a little bit afraid is, wondering what the world can be! Is it but a world of trouble—sadness set to song? Is its beauty but a bubble bound to break ere long? Are its palaces and pleasures fantasies that fade? And the glory of its treasures shadow of a shade? School-girls we, eighteen and under, from scholastic trammels free, and we wonder—how we wonder!—What on earth the world can be!

∽

When she opens the window she hears a whisper somewhere and running footsteps. Then the sound of the occasional car passing on the street and the voices of the drama girls, carrying through the vents and on the breeze. They're rehearsing *The Mikado*. Of course, these little idiots, too removed from the real world to know that yellowface is offensive. Their parents will love it, though. This is the narrative of racism in neighborhoods like Rosedale, Forest Hill, the Bridle Path: families cushioned by money, too far-removed from life to know they're doing any harm.

There are still so many papers to grade. She hasn't looked at any yet. And she can't imagine finishing them tonight. She doesn't want to imagine finishing them. Sometimes the thought of doing anything for her students fills her with sick dread, the feeling that she should run. The feeling dances inside her now. Scrabbles at her ribs.

She leans on the windowsill, on stiff locked arms. In one hand, the pack of cigarettes. In the other, the lighter. She can almost make out the lyrics of the song. She remembers it from when she was a freshman; she saw *The Mikado* at the Hart House Theatre with Jeff Becker. Where was he now? In the dark he'd held her hand and worked her ring around her finger like he was unscrewing it, that cheap silver ring she'd bought at a jewelry stand in Costa del Sol, run by a pair of hippies who'd also offered her hash. He'd twisted her ring. He'd brushed her thin hair behind her ear. He'd brushed his lips against it.

Let's get out of here, he'd said.

She remembers this: her heartbeat, singing in her ears, mixing with the orchestra. *Getting out of there*: she'd never done that before, couldn't imagine it. How did it feel to get out of there? Did it hurt? What happened afterwards? Would he still like her after they'd got out of there? And her strange mole, the one on her back—he couldn't see that.

The voices of the chorus rose and fell. She thumbed open the pack of cigarettes.

No, let's stay, she'd said. Her damp armpits: she'd noticed them then. She'd turned to him, his frown. *I want to watch this.*

She'd fumbled with something in her hand—her ring? Something else?—like she fumbled the lighter now. Anything to get her hand out of his. The chorus really was beautiful, she'd thought then. She'd willed herself to think it. She thought it now. The high, tinkling voices. The fluttering kimonos, modest and bright.

HOW DO YOU DEAL WITH THE HORRIBLY CRUEL THINGS PEOPLE HAVE SAID TO YOU THROUGHOUT YOUR LIFE?

I like to make people out of walnuts. Grandmaw taught me. She had a bag full of plastic feet and another full of googly eyes. She said, you just glue the feet on the bottom of the nut like so. Then you put on two eyes. And sometimes you jazz up your nut, add a bit of yarn for hair or some funny little pipe cleaner arms. Look how they bend.

Nut accessories are fancier now. Used to be the only kind of feet you could get for a walnut were bare feet, but now at a good craft store you can get little shoes. Also, tiny hats.

I've made thousands of nut people. Every one has its own personality. Cowboy nuts. Spaceman nuts. This is a nun nut, here.

This is my family. Grandmaw, rest her. With a little apron. Grandpaw, rest him too. His hair's a cotton ball. Mawmaw in a pink sunhat, and my brother with a dog. Pawpaw's got a golf club in his pipe cleaner hand. I made these as presents for them, actually, which was stupid. Really just I don't know why I did that. Pawpaw said he never played golf, which was so true, and therefore this nut didn't look like him at all, and then everybody else admitted their nuts were garbagey. And what kind of fuckwit would want nuts like this besides someone like me who loves them, right? So, I keep them hidden away here. They're probably the worst nuts I've ever made but I've made lots of better ones since, like this congressman nut.

All I know is I have to keep making them, gluing the pieces together, trying to finally get them right. Sometimes I do it without thinking. Look, I'm making one now.

ANY LITTLE MORSEL

When she had no food left in the house and no more will to eat, Helen cannibalized her manuscripts. She started with the recipes: *Aunt Florence's Blue-Ribbon Bundt Cake, Golda Meir's Chicken Soup, Bacon Bite Cornbread.* These she had published, some time ago, in the *Ladies' Home Journal.* Now they were carbon copies slid out of old manila hanging files that had stoicized in her filing cabinet since 1969.

Her first attempts were primitive. She cut the recipes apart with kitchen scissors, separated each ingredient into its own neat strip, and masticated them until they were pulpy and warm. Then she swallowed, each sharp directive and thick noun meeting inside her until she'd pulped the recipe into a gluey gruel, cooked it in her pickled old stomach as in a cauldron. She survived like this, for a time. And when she didn't eat words, she read them: every page of the *New York Times,* from the headlines to the classifieds to the crosswords, which she filled out in ink.

Her daughter phoned long distance out of a sense of duty or guilt. She asked, flat voiced, *What are you eating?*

Checkerboard Square Clam Crunch, said Helen, voice heavy with phlegm. She double-folded the newspaper in her lap, filled in another space in the crossword. *Tomato Stuffed with Perfection Salad. Hamburger-Olive Loaf, and, just today, Truffle Trout Aspic.*

And her daughter wondered at her mother's ability to cook, considering Helen's talent for wreckage. Wondered, but didn't much care.

What Helen's recipes provided in nourishment they lacked in flavor. They had the piquancy of Campbell's soup labels and the texture of wallpaper. Helen hungered for stronger words.

She began on the lifestyle articles. Anecdotes about raising three children in the 1950s, about dinner parties and leading Girl Scout meetings and Daniel's boxcar built to look like a pirate ship, all snipped to bits. She ingested her children, one by one. Their antics, which had looked so delightful on the pages of the *Omaha World Herald*, all slipped down her gullet: first Robin, then Ann. Daniel, always the favorite, she saved for last. She scissored the yellowed newsprint into pasta and wound it around an unwashed fork. She folded her carbons into tea sandwiches and sucked on their corners until they were soft enough to tear off small bites. She layered them into patties and doused them in Worcestershire sauce.

When her children were gone, she eased herself into her rocker and folded her brittle hands over her gut, satisfied. The consumption of each name seemed to give her back something of herself. Her flesh clung to her bones a little tighter. She felt old youth snaking through her once more: a warmth that began in her heart and spread out to each dangling limb like the warmth of a gulp of wine or a long draw off a cigarette.

Most intoxicating was the flood of ambition: a feeling she had enjoyed many decades ago, before much of what made her Helen had happened. It was heady and rich and made her drunk with herself. It was something she had to have. She ate her high school diploma, granted her when she was only fourteen. She ate the angry letters she wrote her father, the ones he'd refused to open, the ones that begged him to send her to college: the ones she'd saved for no reason she could fathom; perhaps she had known she'd digest them one day. She ate her certificate from secretarial school and her membership certificate from Job's Daughters and her marriage certificate and all else she could find. She ate it all and it was gone.

She steamed all of her correspondence in a giant double boiler and soaked it with vinegar and slathered it with mustard before scarfing it down. Rejection letters were glassy cabbage leaves. Letters from family were bland and perfunctory potatoes. Her husband Robert's letters, sometimes fat and witty, sometimes biting, sometimes cruel and drunk and gone bad, were the meat around which the whole meal was based.

When those were gone, Helen was herself again. She unmothballed her old hats and gloves and dresses. She began to go on short outings to the mall and drives down Saddle Creek and through Benson, twisting through the old neighborhoods in her ancient Karmann Ghia.

It was around this time that Helen received a letter from her granddaughter. Too young to compose something original, she'd copied letters Helen had written her mother in months prior. *Please send pictures*. She drew a picture of herself. And Helen, who had not been the subject of a photo in at least ten years, drove to Target in floppy brimmed hat and costume jewelry and elbow-length gloves, her face clotted with powder and dots of rouge and coral lips. She sat in a photo booth and pressed her gloved hand to her face and kissed for the camera five times, each pose almost identical to the pose in the preceding photo. She mailed the photo strip to her granddaughter in her last envelope, and then ate the letter her young granddaughter had sent.

After eating all of her other compositions, Helen was left with one small, locked drawer of manuscripts, right under the lip of her roll top desk. For days, she contemplated the key to the drawer. It had sat in the bottom of her jewelry box for decades, getting dark and green. Now its ring dangled from her gloved finger as she floated around the apartment looking for things to do, ways to distract herself. But there was nothing.

Helen remembered what was in the drawer. Dwelled on it. Fantasized about it. What was in the drawer was pure and rare and aged now like a fine wine kept for years in a cellar: poems. All had been written in the small, now distant window between leaving home and meeting Robert, all unpublished but still full of youth and promise. All, undoubtedly, delicious. But Helen didn't want to devour them in one meal. She wanted to rediscover them, savor them over time like an epicurean with delectables, read and reread them, ingest them word by word. She feared she might not have the willpower.

Her skin was again growing loose and hung close to her bones. The only nourishment in the apartment called to her until she finally gave in, turned the key in the lock, held the brittle yellowed manuscripts in her hands like giant water crackers, collapsed in her chair with them, pored over them. They were plucky bits of flapper verse, all set in the Gold Coast. About driving to and from parties, drunken rooftop sunrises, ill-fated pairings among Omaha's debauched youth. They reeked of optimism. They were bad, Helen knew. But they were hers. Their smell was mildew and wood with top notes of ribbon ink and old fruitiness. She wanted to melt them between her tongue and the roof of her mouth. She wanted to absorb them back into herself and feel the old youth again.

She began by scissoring them carefully into delicate words, most small as grains of rice. Then she poured them into a dusty Fiestaware bowl, minding their presentation. She balanced the bowl on her lap and her bird-thin hand hovered above it, fingers twitching. She plucked a word from the bowl and hurried it into her mouth.

It tasted even better than she'd imagined. Like fine hors d'oeuvres, or candies she remembered from childhood, or something even more essential to her survival that she couldn't quite place. She let it linger in her mouth for a moment. Then it slipped down her throat and warmed every part of her as nothing else had ever done. She was twenty-one again. She could do a dance if she wanted to. She could smash all the bottles in the apartment and crush her cigarettes under her slippered feet. She slipped another word into her mouth.

By the time evening fell, she was scraping the bottom of the bowl for '*a*'s and '*the*'s: any little morsel. She had consumed all the poems in one ecstatic rush and now the dim light that came moments after sunset blued the unlit apartment. Helen stood alone in her living room. The charge of youth began to drain from her old body and was gone as quickly as it had come. She hadn't had the willpower to save what was good, to tend it and make it last. She'd thought she'd be more disappointed. But now, after taking back all of her old self, she had no regrets. She would stop eating altogether. This would be dignified.

Her daughter phoned and asked, *What are you eating?*
Leftovers, said Helen.
And her daughter didn't ask any questions.

Helen's dignity lasted four days. Then she began to cringe from hunger. She craved more words. She couldn't fight the cravings; they doubled her over in pain. Defeated, she dragged her old Olivetti out of a closet and set it up on a card table in the kitchen. She'd begin to compose again. She fed the Olivetti and her bird hands hovered over the keys. But no ideas came to her. She sat in front of the blank page for an hour. At last, she typed her own name at the top corner of the sheet, tore it off and slipped it into her mouth. The bitter new paper hardly satisfied her.

Every day she returned to the typewriter. But the words never came. Helen grew hungrier. Her old anger returned. She was a pathetic animal, waiting to feed. She nibbled at the newspaper, but it provided no sustenance.

Finally, to stave off the deepest emptiness, she ate crosswords: a quick fix, the puzzles at the back of the *Omaha World Herald*. She completed them in ten minutes and snipped them apart and ate her penciled-in words in five. For longer words she ate from the *New York Times* crossword. She could finish it in twenty-five minutes, even on a Sunday: a feat that had always amazed Robert, and her father when she was a girl. But even that more substantial crossword gave her single words, thin and meatless like potato chips. An old woman couldn't survive on them. Before long, Helen had only the strength to fetch the paper from her doorstep and fill out the crosswords. And soon enough she didn't have the strength for that. She sat in her living room chair, immobile, with an eaten crossword on her lap. She stared at it and it stared back at her, wordless.

A BIRD
OF UNCERTAIN
ORIGIN

Its story is the boy who kneels to see what he's shot: beak parted, feet curled.

This is 1900. This is at the edge of a thirsty cornfield. The sky is grey. The bird is grey with blots of red and blue. The day is a cool March day enveloped by other cool March days.

Its story is the boy's mother. She strokes it as she'd stroke the hair of a feverish child. *I was your age last time I saw one like this. People said they were all gone.* She wears a deep sadness the boy has not seen in his lifetime.

The boy's creeping feelings, the melt where there once was pride: this is the bird's story, too. He watches his mother wrap the bird in rags and put it in a shoebox, whisper to it. *We'll find a home for you.* That night, he turns in his narrow bed.

This is where the carcass of the last wild passenger pigeon goes: a museum in Columbus. The woman who's prepared the bird has thick arms like bolster pillows. She guides the boy and his mother to where she's perched the bird.

I used shoe buttons for the eyes, she says. *We call him Buttons now.*

This is not the last wild passenger pigeon: overstuffed, with a dull unlidded look that betrays no secrets. It's under a glass box that throws back the boy's own reflection.

And this is suddenly and forever in the boy: the living bird, still high in the tree where he sighted it. He feels it gazing out his own eyes like through a thicket. He feels its head cock at the sight of itself. He thinks he might even feel it sigh.

Soon, he will never know his own heartbeat from a flapping of wings.

THE BONES
OF JACQUES AND FRANÇOIS

They came snuffled out of the earth by pigs. First the long femurs, then delicate hand bones drifted apart over time. The skulls were last to surface. Both missing their lower jaws, so they might never speak.

Christophe lifted them from their shallow burial place and sent the pigs away with loud claps. British guards watched as he stared into the eye-hollows and tried to tell if the skulls were French. If they had served Napoleon, like him, or if these bones were still loyal to Ferdinand and Isabel of Spain, or to some other nation that had made war with England, in some other time. If they had spent many years in this camp, like him, or if they'd died upon arrival. *Either way,* he thought, *you are Jacques and François,* and he collected up what bones he could.

His captors watched and called him back from the edge of the camp. There was promise of stew. There was a card game. Why had he taken these bones from their grave?

Christophe looked long at the bones he'd bundled in his own shabby coat. He didn't know. The bones had asked to go with him. That was all.

But the bones asked more. They asked to be boiled, the way a soup bone might be boiled. Christophe quietly boiled them. They asked to be set out in the sun so they could bleach white. Christophe set them out side by side. The other prisoners watched Christophe with questions in their eyes. The guards noticed, too. *Alright, Christophe? Ça va?* They asked, with familial concern. Christophe nodded yes.

The bones asked to be carved. Christophe divided them into pieces. Some long slivers and some ornate. One a figurehead. One a mast. He'd had no design when he started, but soon had all the parts for a ship, which fit together like they'd been cut to a blueprint. They needed little glue. For the rigging, Christophe braided strands of his own long hair. For the sails, he used tissue paper. For the flags, he cut shreds from his own retired uniform. To his surprise, the flags were British.

Men crowded around the model ship. Prisoners and guards, both, admired its scrollwork and its latticed windows and its pleasing shape. A small lever in its side brought the cannons out, and the pulleys could be worked with careful fingers to raise the sails.

By God, it's the H.M.S. Victory, said one of the guards.

More skeletons surfaced by way of pigs, and Christophe duly gathered them. Now his fellow inmates helped boil and bleach the bones, and carved them at Christophe's direction while the guards looked on. Sometimes even a guard would sit and carve for a time, with Christophe showing him where to bend the pieces to make the hull, and how to carve a flower into a window frame. It made the days pass.

Over months, the prisoners of war assembled the whole British fleet. A fleet of bone that gleamed in what dim light it could catch. And word of the small fleet, of the ships' fine-tuned construction and the cleverness of their workings, reached British Naval Officers who lived nearby. They clamored to collect them.

So the Commandant of the camp arranged a sale, whereby prisoners could earn income from their crafts. Some sold wooden furniture and some tapestries sewn from cast-off thread, and these fetched a fair price from civilians. But the officers came for the ships of bone. Christophe negotiated their sale with a merchant's shrewd spirit. One hook-nosed officer said he was buying a ship for Admiral Nelson, which would sit in his office amid leather-bound books and maps of the seas and fine marble busts and medals of honor.

And the ships were gone. Sailed off, as on the ocean. Christophe divided his profit among the men who'd helped make the ships, even the guards. The ship-making men enjoyed an evening of good Alsatian wine and songs played on concertina, and it was the most enjoyment they'd had since being brought to camp.

But, after the hundreds of hours he'd spent with them, Christophe missed the ships. He wondered how he had known to prepare and build them. In what obscure corner of his mind had the schematics of every ship in the British fleet been buried? How had he known to take the bones? What of the pigs, who'd tromped over the same grave a thousand times before and never nosed it? And Jacques and François, and the many men whose bones had surfaced, what would they think now, being transformed into small vessels of war?

These questions had no answers, concluded Christophe. There was no use thinking of them.

Only later did stories reach camp of the devastation the ships had wrought in the libraries and curio cabinets of the English. As if the models were possessed, the cannons extended of their own accord and fired a series of tiny missiles from their port and starboard sides. Several books and artworks took critical hits, including a marble bust of George III whose nose was knocked away. Documents of great import were pocked with holes. Entire battle plans were ruined, with Admiral Nelson's secretary reporting significant damage to maps and campaign plans. The Lord Admiral himself had sustained a black eye, and banished the ship to the rubbish heap, ordering it to be smashed to smithereens. Taking the Admiral's lead, the English were smashing the ships posthaste. Many ships had already been hurled into ponds and rivers. One was angrily plunged into a spa.

And Christophe? This was where he spent the next several months: in the Black Hole, shackled to the wall next to an old, yellow-bearded rigger from Napoleon's fleet whose eyes rode crazily in their sockets. The man had been in the Black Hole so long he couldn't remember the year. Every day a guard came to give the men their rations. Every day the guard joked that Christophe wouldn't see meat on the bone for the rest of his time at camp. And every day the old rigger dragged breath in and out of himself with a clatter like chains dragged over rocks. This man's noise might have been enough to break Christophe, but he stayed stoic, did not cry out at all until the old man, suffering some fever, collapsed across his lap, declared he was dying, and begged Christophe to make a fine ship, one that could blow a hole clear through Wellington's knackers, out of his own old bones. Christophe promised he would.

But he didn't. By the time he was released from the Black Hole all the pigs had been eaten and the earth in the burial ground remained unturned. Instead of pigs, a dumb flock of geese.

Christophe spent the rest of the war playing cards and learning to read. Sometimes, between card games or during walks around the camp, he watched the geese waddle across the lawn.

Their strange formation and their white feathers. The geese pecked and honked and bobbed through the yard, over the burial places of Jacques and François and the old rigger. Then they spread further out, over all the unnamed who had died as prisoners, like ghost-white ships on a great green sea.

THE GARNET CAVE

The garnet cave belonged to the children, and only the children could go there. She learned this from the children themselves, who volunteered the information on the first day of school. *Do you know about our cave?* they asked. *Has anyone told you?*

This was in Alaska, a town nestled into a wrinkle in the coastline. This was her first job, this teaching job, in this tiny town, in Alaska, where weather had sanded the storefronts down to soft grey clapboard.

Soon enough she saw the children—the same ones she taught on weekdays—selling garnets on Saturdays and Sundays. They set up tables in front of houses and on the roadside, laid them with cloth and scattered the garnets over the cloth like craft sequins: mottled browns and tans that caught the scrimshaw-white sun, deep, throbbing reds that seemed to breathe like tiny animals. Some garnets small as crumbs and some the size of her knuckle. When she touched them, they were warm between her fingers.

She began to buy garnets. She left some on her nightstand and some in every pocket. The town got darker every day, sun easing into its long hibernation. When she walked alone in the dark, she would put her hands in her pockets and feel the warmth of secret stones. Sometimes, between school bells, she sneaked a hand into her pocket for comfort.

Her old landlady, Mrs. Evert, was the first to notice. *You have your pockets full, don't you?* She folded the rent check into a square, tucked it into a corner of her patent leather purse. Then she opened her purse wide, as wide as it would go, and grinning inside its satin-lined mouth were a thousand glittering garnet teeth. *We all do, you know. I collected these, myself, as a girl.*

And it was true: every adult in town carried garnets. This was true of fishermen and true of shopkeepers and true of realtors and true of nurses and true of reeling drunks. Some had so many garnets they spilled them wherever they went: garnets tumbling from loose seams, garnets tucked into hatbands. Some had only a few, held in pouches around their necks or in pillboxes. There was an old man, as ancient and carved as a totem pole, who sat all day in a folding chair in front of the grocery store, peering into the deep red heart of a single garnet.

She learned that adults did not like to be asked about their garnets, and very few offered to show theirs to her. They looked at her sideways in stores and in restaurants. They greeted her on the street and quickly kept moving, clutching their garnets to themselves, in pocket or bag. They were years older than her, or they had families, or they were only in town for a short visit. This made her clutch her own garnets tighter. This made her long for home.

She began to ask questions of the children. *How did you get the garnet cave?*

It's always belonged to the kids. For as long as the town's been a town.

What does it look like? Is it beautiful?

The children looked at each other, shrugged.

Would I be able to find it, if I went out with a map?

No. You'd never find it with a map. They laughed. *Every grown up asks us that.*

But haven't most of the grown-ups here been there, when they were kids?

Meek nods all around. *But they forget.*

The children knew many secret places. After school, she'd watch them move away like a murmuration of starlings, fan out between buildings and down alleyways, rejoin somewhere out of sight. She could hear their clamor rise up beyond the squat business district. This noise, too, seemed to hold a secret; it rose and fell like the definite tide, hushing up, every night, over the town's pebbled beach.

Sometimes she followed the children. She knew this was wrong. She'd trail them, soft, to the places they gathered. She'd watch them from around corners and behind trees. She'd clutch her pocketed garnets and try to burrow into the children's whispers. She never made out the words.

And, at school, the children watched her with little smiles painted on their faces, like they knew exactly what she was about. Had they seen her, she wondered? But they only handed in their work or raised their hands and answered questions. They never questioned her.

In town people went about their business as if she were hardly there. At the grocery store she stared into an old man's single garnet, and he squeezed it away in his veiny grip. She began to walk at night, alone.

That was when she saw them on the edge of the water, filling an aluminum rowboat with pails and sandwiches and flashlights. Three or four children climbed into the boat: some she knew by name, some she recognized from the schoolyard. When they were seated, four or five more appeared and piled in, then another bunch, until the rowboat sat so low that only its lip protruded. Two manned the oars and the boat groaned along the inlet. She watched from behind a dry-docked fishing boat as the small silhouettes moved farther away. When they were distant enough, she emerged to watch them slip between two outcroppings of rock. Their voices carried back to her like waves palpating the shore.

And she followed, in a twin rowboat that waited for her on the pebbles. Its aluminum gleamed in the moonlight. Its oars fit snug into her grip, and the boat skated through the inlet even though she hardly rowed. She followed the children's voices. Occasionally, she'd see their boat slip through a pass ahead. Once, she thought she saw a glance in her direction, heard a harsh whisper.

Then the children's voices ghosted apart, some to the other side of the inlet, some back to shore, some down to the water and many straight up to the sky, painting it fantastic green like emeralds and blue like sapphires and purple, like the garnets they gathered. Laughter drifted up towards the stars in soft curls; yelps sent spikes of color across the palette of the sky; whispers were bluegreen billows. She sat in the rowboat, watching the play of lights and voices in the sky, and their twins on the water.

Heavy quiet fell and rested on everything. With no sun to anchor her she drifted in time. When she looked back, she couldn't see the beach. When she looked ahead, the rocks of the inlet had melted into the water. When she looked up, the sky was black. Her heart thumped like the deep pulsing of the garnets. The children were gone. She was lost. She put down her oars. It was so dark she couldn't be sure whether her eyes were open or closed.

And in that deep stillness, she saw the garnet cave.

Daylight. Children climbed rock faces cluttered with garnets. Children tore through paths of loose garnets like gravel.

Around the mouth of the cave, children ate wild blueberries, salmonberries, cloudberries. They played, and they stripped off their coats and swam in the icy water. They sang ancient songs of childhood. They wore clothes for all seasons. Some wore waistcoats and some wore skins and some wore tee shirts.

A velveteen feeling came from the garnet cave. She remembered this feeling well. When she let it take her, she noticed children she knew: Mrs. Evert, her smooth young face like a seal's, filling a toy purse with garnets. The school principal, poking a garnet into his little ear. The old man from the grocery store, tiny and towheaded, staring deep into the heart of the very same garnet.

A new child emerged from around the margin of a crag: herself, in a dress made by her mother, bent over a pool in a rock, disturbing the water with her small fingers. She lifted a garnet from the pool: twin to one she clutched, now, in her pocket. For a moment, she held it up to the light. Refracted back at her, the ancient wisdom of her childhood. How could she ever have forgotten?

She must leave herself here, she understood, like all the children must leave themselves; it was the price of living. Tomorrow, the children she'd seen in the boat would be in school, yes, but different, dreaming of different compass points, clutching their own garnets away, not knowing the way back to the cave, just like her.

THE STORIES YOU WRITE ABOUT MIMICO

One—Oscar Peterson's Piano is Out of Tune

And he's strolling—back and forth, back and forth—before a bank of impressive windows that look out from his penthouse in the Amedeo Court Apartments. He is alone. But, if you were there, Bess, you could lean an elbow on the empty bar and watch him silhouette himself against Lake Ontario, that old body of water. She's gray today, smoker gray. Like he takes his cues from nature, Oscar Peterson stuffs and lights his pipe. Silky coils of smoke curve from his nostrils, the corners of his mouth, to gather in a cloud above his head. Across Humber Bay, smokestacks. The CN Tower, blinking, red-eyed.

Where's his wife? Don't ask questions. Oscar Peterson just wants to play the piano right now. He wants to knock some sense back into the world, key by key. Sometimes you just have to make music, because music is the only thing that stays, isn't it? Music can't lie, music can't be disappointed in you.

Oscar Peterson is on the phone again, with the piano tuners. He called three hours ago. They promised to be here within the hour. He shouldn't have to do this. He shouldn't have to pick up the telephone today. Somehow, it's wrong in his hand, the soulless touchtone with its tangled cord. It should be a big shiny receiver to bellow into, a heavy and rewarding rotary dial that yields to his finger, whirrs back into place.

Oscar Peterson is eating a snack. He sits at the Steinway and tucks into whatever this is—leftovers? Something he made and froze, before he went on tour. He'd never allow this, normally: food at the piano. But, now. He tests out a little something, just a little scale. Maybe it's not so bad, maybe he can just sit here and play while he waits.

But the mid-range is unbearable. Like a rake on his brain! Like a witch's hand, plunged into his chest, icing his heart with the scratch of a fingernail. How can he still be waiting? How is it possible the piano has gone out of tune again, in such a short time? At least, it seems like it's been a short time—but it's been months, hasn't it? Months since he's been in Toronto, at all, let alone this apartment. The light slants in nicely here this time in the afternoon. It's been a while since he's noticed that. You can notice it, Bess. It's OK to notice it.

Oscar Peterson sits in silence. For the first time in a long time, he listens to the voice of the lake.

Sssssshhhhhhhh, she whispers. *Sssssssshhhhhhhh*.

Two—A Gift for Mussolini

Two horses, soft-nosed and tall. They are fresh-brushed and shiny. They are hungry and attentive. They poke their heads from their stables to greet the two men who approach with apples.

These men speak Italian; the horses do not, but they take the apples.

One of the men, Mr. Franceschini, is familiar to the horses. You aren't a horse, Bess, but you recognize this man, too, from curious nights spent researching the complex you'd moved to, the strange, hollowed out mansion at the center of it, and its foreboding old gardens peopled with headless putti. The horses know Mr. Franceschini's smell and they know, even now, that he is ill, that every day he grows more and more ill, though he still doesn't know it himself.

Mr. Franceschini comes often to the stables wearing fine riding habits, a tall top hat that reaches up to the horses' ears, and carrying a whip. The horses remember, most, the whip: its snap at the haunches. And sometimes, the top of the hat, which is made of flattened fur, and which shows spooky propellers of light when he leads them to the ring.

Today, Mr. Franceschini does not wear the hat. Perhaps because the other man, the stranger, is not very tall. What the horses notice: the shiny gold buttons on the stranger's breast, his gray coat that smells of elsewhere, his velvet lapel. You may try to make out the stranger, too, Bess, but he's no one you recognize. Some lesser Italian official with a uniform made in Milan. When a horse noses forward to touch its lip to the bill of the stranger's cap, the stranger reaches up and clasps the horse's muzzle, lifts the tender lip to inspect its teeth.

Molto bella.

Now the horses are saddled. Shiny oxblood leather, a smell that means they can expect, next, the cold bit, a man's weight on their backs, the dust of the ring, and the clash of the nearby lake as it kicks the rocky shore.

With the help of a set of stairs, Mr. Franceschini guides the stranger onto the back of one horse while he mounts the other. Imagine yourself here, Bess, perched on the fence. You can watch them trot around the ring. Their astonishing purebred gait. Their mahogany coats, lighting like fire.

This is the ring, to the horses: at one end, the comfortable stables, the sweet smell of hay and sleep and food, and, beyond that, the place where Mr. Franceschini lives, his green-roofed dwelling with its greenhouse that sends off sparks of sunlight, and the little girl, the daughter, Martha, who wears flapping white hair ribbons and plays in the gardens and brings the horses pocketsful of sugar cubes. At the other end, within view, the edge of the ground, the meeting-place between water and land, where Lake Ontario stretches endlessly. The lake smells of strange animals and plants. The lake is a place the horses have never been. Sometimes, at night, when they poke their heads out from the stalls, a spray drifts in carrying its scent of elsewhere. Sometimes that scent is sweet and inviting, like the newest, freshest hay. Sometimes it drifts in as a nightmare, bringing whiffs of the abattoir. They tuck their noses into each other's necks and try to sleep that scent away.

Who would predict the keenness of the stranger's boot heels, and the force and frequency with which he uses them? Incessant kick, kick, kick at the ribs as he urges the horse forward. At the same time, he yanks at the bit.

Mr. Franceschini, noticing this struggle, urges calm. *Loosen up on the bit a touch. Yes, that's the way. And maybe—with greatest respect, Signore—maybe do not dig your heels in so hard, she's very sensitive and well-trained. She knows how to take corners.*

The stranger, ramrod-stiff. *Of course.* He loosens the reins.

But he is offended. Mr. Franceschini does not know this. Stranger and horse cannot connect. Horse feels for stranger, and stranger is—does horse feel this correctly?—not a rider, but some cargo loaded onto her back, simply a machine that urges her forward. She grunts against his tautness, but no-one notices: not the other horse, not Mr. Franceschini. Why won't they notice?

Look, Bess, at the way he rides her. He doesn't bother to post; her trot jars him; he bounces and lands askew. Look at the set of his jaw, so tight. It belongs to a man who believes animals should be broken. If you keep looking, you'll already know how this ends.

Yes, announces the stranger. *She is a very fine gift, indeed.*

At that moment, a commotion: Martha, in only her slip and hair ribbons, come running from the house. The soles of her feet are blackened with dirt. Her mother runs after her. Little girl, climbing over the fence, throwing one leg over, then the other. She's crying. She points at the stranger.

You can't have her!

The stranger notices. The horse notices, too. Turns her head toward the girl. Sugar cube? Warm stables?

Father signals to Mother; Mother grabs at daughter; daughter swats Mother away.

You can't have my horse! she screams.

The stranger grits his teeth. Ticking jaw muscles. A slightly raised eyebrow at this little girl, this brat.

I hate you!

Three—No One Cares for Bauhaus in Toronto

As evidence, just look at the buildings. Soot-blackened, Victorian, and so very Protestant in their proportions. Column, column, always an even number of columns, and dark little windows, always. Andor feels the buildings bearing down on him each time he grinds into the city on the streetcar, on his way to his weekly English lesson.

These lessons taught by a woman named Ruth, whose stockings shush against her rayon skirt when she walks round and round the classroom, peeking over shoulders at her students' work. And the hair! Stiff, sprayed until it is like something Andor might have carved from wood back in Weimar. Ruth, with her pinned-on smile.

That's not fair. Perhaps her smile is genuine. Perhaps this woman truly cares about Andor's essay on his favorite animal. Each week, an essay. Students read their essays aloud, one by one. For this week's assignment, Andor took Cornelia to the High Park Zoo again, on the Long Branch streetcar: the only transportation line he's certain about.

You've been to this zoo hundreds of times, Bess. If you were walking with Andor and Cornelia on that chilly October day in 1952 you might have seen those familiar animals, nosing for food among the fallen leaves: the llama, the sheep, the bison, the deer, the curious peacock. The father and daughter.

Which is your favorite animal? he asked.

Cornelia pointed.

Andor's essay is on the bison. This seems to trouble Ruth.
Really? Of all the animals?

The beard makes him look like a professor, says Andor.

Ruth smiles. *Well, that's different.*

Andor looks around for commiseration, for someone else who loves the bison. Nothing. His classmates have written about the lion, the butterfly, the dove. The beautiful animals. They dutifully read their essays.

Next week's essay assignment: to describe his home, his street.

There is a stop to make today, before going home: Simpson's department store, that great brown edifice at the corner of Yonge and Queen, with its big avenues lit by sconces and its perfume ladies, always reaching over counters. This is a poor substitute for Warenhaus Tietz or, dare he think of it, Le Bon Marché. Everything so held back here. The whole store is tentatively decorated with jack-o-lanterns and black-and-orange bunting. You'll remember this store from childhood, Bess, its green SIMPSON'S sign announcing itself. The pleasing curve of the *S*. Long after the store went out of business your grandmother saved the plastic bags, neatly folded into a drawer.

Here is his destination: ABSTRACTS AT HOME. A series of mock rooms made up in the modern style, meant to nudge Canadian living rooms into the middle of the century. Here we find hairpin legs on streamlined tables; tight, geometrical upholstery in green and yellow and red tweeds. The starburst clock. In each room, an abstract painting.

The paintings are what Andor looks at now, hands clasped behind his back as he paces from room to room, stopping before each one. This group of artists will go on to become the famed Canadian abstractionists the Painters Eleven—but Andor doesn't know that yet. All he knows is Jack Bush's thick ribbons of paint in oranges and greys and blues. Tom Hodgson's color palettes stolen from the sunset, orange and purple and gold. Kazuo Nakamura's stick-straight lines and abstracted trees. And, of course, the aggressive work of young William Ronald—blood splats, like varicose veins around a bruise or wound. This, in particular, makes a feeling in Andor. What is the feeling? Anger? No. This, the very shape of this splat of paint: this is the feeling of betrayal.

What had William said? *We've got to have this one in the show.*

A show in a department store? The idea had seemed crass, but William was so keen on it as he explained the idea that

Andor simply smiled and offered another cup of coffee. Alright, he would exhibit in this show. So hard, it was, to get any attention at all here in Toronto. *People have to see your work,* William had said.

This was in Andor's small studio space, by the window of his snug rented living room on Norris Crescent. The sun had slanted in just then, illuminating William's young broad face as he'd admired one of Andor's crisp shape paintings, its body-like figures so full of energy they almost leaped off the canvas. This was a skill Andor had learned at the Bauhaus, under Kandinsky, who had lectured on color theory in a voice so authoritative that Andor was sure, then, he'd begun to see new and altogether more beautiful colors. This anecdote he'd told William that afternoon, and William had paid rapt attention, asking question after question about Andor's mentorship under Kandinsky and Klee and Moholy-Nagy. Young William, so impressionable. He'd only just graduated from the Ontario College of Art, which Andor had thought a rather gray technical school when William had taken him to the student exhibition. *You are the only one with any talent,* Andor had said then.

Now, in the home section of Simpson's, he regrets that admission.

May I help you, Sir?

This is a furniture salesman.

I look at the paintings.

Different, aren't they? asks the salesman. There's a pride to the question, as if he's painted these works himself.

Andor grinding home on the Queen streetcar. Figures, clothed in grey fabric, strolling on the gray sidewalk. Above Toronto, a gray blanket of sky. Here come the first snowflakes of the season, testing the air. Andor, in the streetcar, pushes west and west and west.

Here is Andor's stop. Now he is walking down his street, Norris Crescent, with its low brown hipped-roof duplexes lined up like houses in a toy village. You know the feeling of walking down Norris Crescent, Bess, when it's empty of people and the wind churns up from the lake. Little snowflakes pelting the eyes. You can slip between buildings and through the alley and wind up in your apartment building, the one being constructed, now, on the old Martha Villa property, as Andor mounts the steps to his duplex. Cornelia is at the window. She presses her palms against the glass.

Andor must sit down and write a letter to William, expressing his deep disappointment. Why was he not included? Why, after their conversations? After the encouragement he'd given?

And, yes, there is something else he must write. It nags at the back of his brain. Vision of Ruth, with sprayed hair and pinned-on smile. An essay. He has a week to write it. *My home. My street.*

Four—No One Who Played with The Rolling Stones Ever Lived on Norris Crescent

This is you, Bess, hauling the first boxes into the elevator of your new building in Amedeo Court. In one arm, a box teetering dangerously; in the other, the basset hound's leash. He sniffs the carpet, tests a soiled patch with a lick. The elevator, midcentury, jitters as it rises. Its gold paint is flaking. It smells like cigarettes and skin and mushroom gravy.

This is your mom, arranging the unpacked boxes into shapes. A table-shape, a wall-shape. A week has passed since you moved in, and she refuses to unpack the boxes, just makes more shapes. *We'll be moving out of here soon,* she says.

Her one concession to the setting: the little bell she's hung out on the balcony, to be teased by the lake wind. Wind teases the bell all the time.

Is this better or worse than living in the car? In the car, the landscape flung itself past and past, going from brown to green to snowy to hot. In the car, you could end up in Charleston or Des Moines or Niagara Falls or Halifax or Ithaca. In the car, possibility lay ahead, at the end of some road you hadn't taken yet. You were with your mom and your dog and all your things were in storage, and the old house was behind you, not lost but something you'd chosen to leave. Now, back in Toronto, the old house is over there—way over there, in a neighborhood you can't afford. It's not yours anymore, but—you think about this sometimes, at night—it still contains millions of your cells, and maybe the marks on the inside of your closet where you re-corded your height every year. Also, the place inside the closet where, twelve years old, you wrote, light light in pencil, *fuck.*

This is Mimico, where you live now: the old Polish bakery and the old motels and the tumbledown storefronts hung with plastic torsos that flap in the wind. A drunk stumbles out of the Blue Goose Tavern and into the 7-11. At night, scream-ing fights leave scars on the pavement, an errant high heeled shoe, a puddle from where bloody nose met sidewalk. Along the shore, manmade outcroppings of rock host little bonfires. Around the bonfires, on camp chairs and recliners taken from curbs and dumpsters, silhouettes of people. They raise bottles of beer and paper cups of coffee to their mouths. No one seems to stop this practice, the lakeside camps of homeless and addicted. Sometimes, by day, they call out to you as you walk the dog, call him a good boy, raise their bottles. They are always nice to you. A thought—bad thought: does this make you one of them? There are certain drunks you recognize, will come, even, to love: Michael, who will die of a horrific tumor on his lip;

the old man with the Chihuahua that rides on his walker. The old man smiles and smiles.

The lake is a character, here, too. It waves grayly. Beyond it, the Toronto skyline: the ever-multiplying condo buildings, glass and flashing steel, and the shell of the SkyDome and the CN Tower always, you've thought, looking the colors of a boot sock: gray, with a collar of white and red.

Here are the water birds. Ducks and geese and swans and others that visit from distant countries and climates. A small preserve set aside for them, with nesting areas and a wooden boardwalk that's bouncy underfoot. Later, when you lose the car, can't afford to get it out of the garage it's been towed to, you'll walk the boardwalk with a heavy IKEA bag filled with the week's groceries: cans and crinkly bags of veg and carefully planned cuts of meat. The lake wind will slap you across the face, making tears streak down.

On these walks, you and your mom will name the water birds. The new crop of goslings, or strange black birds with spoonbills and oily-looking wings. Henrietta. Nicholas. Ryan Gosling.

⁓

Even five months, six months, seven months later, you still live among boxes. You arrange them into makeshift walls, section off the part of the living room that contains your desk. This is your study, itself like a giant cardboard box. Sometimes you do your schoolwork here. Other times, you write.

Writing, maybe, an escape. Only, your stories are bad. No feeling, everything that's real choked off and aborted midway. All ideas and buzzing thoughts meant to push yourself away from yourself. You can't imagine ever being a good writer, ever writing a good story or being anywhere else than here, in your box, in the Amedeo Court apartments, in Mimico, where you'd never invite your old friends. You want to write *fuck* on a box, light light in pencil. You do, and you erase it, and it leaves a dirty smudge.

A neighbor says famous people lived here. This is on Norris Crescent, with its little co-op of brown duplexes, where you walk the dog. The neighbor ashes her cigarette on the metal handrail of her stoop.

In your building, she says. *Oscar Peterson. The jazz guy.*

That can't be right. Not Oscar Peterson. Not in our building, where a shirtless guy daily sits on his balcony, points his amp at the lake, and strums his electric guitar.

Yes, Oscar Peterson. In the penthouse. She squints up at the penthouse, points the glowing tip of her cigarette at it. *That used to be a real fancy building.*

The dog tugs at his leash, whines.

Another guy lived on this street here, too, says the neighbor. *I think he played with the Rolling Stones.*

Here is your new hobby: after your mom goes to bed, you sit in your cardboard box and research the people who lived here before. Does it surprise you to find out it's true, Oscar Peterson lived here? It does. You didn't think much of that neighbor, before. You thought she might be lying, or maybe she just didn't know what she was talking about. But here is a passing mention of his penthouse at Amedeo Court, just a sentence or two. All you know of the penthouse is the extra button in the elevator. You need to turn a key in a special lock when you press the button. The keyhole is unusually round. Oscar Peterson must have carried an unusually round key.

Leaves skitter along the boardwalk. Ducklings now ducks. Skinny fires on rocky outcroppings leap at the November sky. Voices carry far in this air, thin and crisp. Bottles clink. In your

IKEA bag, straps slung over your shoulders like a backpack, potatoes. Ramen noodles.

Your mom sees junk in the preserve. Plastic pop bottles, straws, napkins, floating on some foamy stuff like soap, dangerously near the nesting area.

This is a protected zone, she says. She leans over the railing. The top of her knit cap flaps over her forehead. *I can't believe people.* Now she slings one leg over the railing, now the other. Now she's edging along the beach.

You're not allowed in there, you call. Are people looking? Ducks scatter as your mother tiptoes toward the edge of the water, an intruder as unwelcome as the bottles.

The IKEA bag shrugs low on your shoulders.

Your mom, picking up garbage, pinching it between two fingers. She gathers as much as she can while you glance left and right, hoping no one will notice her. Now she's trudging her way up the bank with an armful of wet junk.

Help me, she says.

∽

No one who played with the Rolling Stones ever lived on Norris Crescent, not as far as you can tell. The only person of any note who ever lived there was a Hungarian artist who seemed to hate Toronto even more than you do now. Here's a little article in the Toronto *Star* about him, his little duplex on Norris, his studies at the Bauhaus right before the Nazis broke it up, scattered its students and teachers across the world. You find a small collection of his art online. It's held in museums. Here, in a New York collection, his sketch of the lakeshore—*your* lakeshore—in bright pastels. Here is an angular sailboat like a water bird, its captain a maddened person-shape, eyes big and terrified.

And here are the old letters—*MV*—welded into the iron fence that surrounds Amedeo Court. Sometimes, when you walk the dog, you come across a set of them. MV, you learn, for Martha Villa, the early 20th-century house at the center of the place, once achingly grand, now chopped up into apartments. Here's an old photo of the family: proud Italian father with merino suit and pomade-slick hair, demure Scottish mother with hands folded around the dumpling-plump baby, Martha, bald and dressed in white christening gown. Martha, privileged child, once loved so very much that everything from here to the lake was hers.

The letters are rusty now. Dilapidated, like so much else on the property. Its mossy garden, its dry fountain full of spitting stone frogs, its crumbling stone walls. Its old stables, now garages that, when open, reveal the butts of trucks. When you walk the dog past, men in the garages cast spooky glances.

∽

You try to write a story about that, the men in garages. It doesn't go so well. Neither does your story about hauling groceries in a heavy sack, about the weight of the cans and the thinness of the straps on tender shoulders. Nothing happens in that story. Your protagonist—a thinly-veiled version of you—contemplates life for a while, the unfairness of it, has a long walk, gets home, is tired, lies down and lets the difficulty of it all just buzz through her body. There is no change. You don't know how to make change happen.

But you know how to lean over the railing and look at the new ducklings. Here they are, children of last year's crop, furrowing their way through the water where, last fall, your mom fished for garbage. Now you hear music: the tinkling of piano keys. A gentle melody, floating down from a place you can't identify. Some condo, maybe. Some fancy party in some glass and steel monstrosity.

You're sure you've heard this song before, the cool way it pirouettes and steps across the air, patters all around like natty raindrops. *Stormy weather*. Yes, that's it. These notes simple and elegant, clear as facts, sometimes lanky and pulled out like a loosened tie. First *Stormy Weather*, then *Angel Eyes*.

Five—Toronto Brings Me No Joy

This the sign-off on Andor's first letter of the day, addressed to an old Bauhaus friend in New York. Andor draws an angular figure in the corner: himself, in a despairing pose. He folds the letter, tucks it into its envelope, affixes the stamp. Everyone in New York is succeeding. Right now, they are having well-received shows of their work, talking and laughing at art openings, eating caviar, surrounded by Americans who respect the Bauhaus, the abstract figures and lines and colors. They're selling their work for outrageous prices, he imagines, living in flats in the Upper West Side. But, not Andor. Still he waits and waits for his visa, and every day spent waiting is a thousand years.

Eva in the corner of the living room, putting on her lipstick in front of a little hanging mirror. She interviews, this afternoon, at Eaton's department store—ironically, across the street from Simpson's. She has practiced her English on Andor all week—*Hello, Sir, how may I help you? That will be four-ninety-five. Would you like a receipt?* Eva is altogether too elegant to work in a place that sells both silk stockings and washing machines. In Weimar, she studied cabinet making. Glorious, avant-garde creations in walnut. She used to recite poetry. Her father—her terrifying father—was a champion fencer. He had a deep scar on his cheek. Why think of this now? What does the scar matter?

I'm going now, she says. *Wish me luck.*

Good luck.

Remember Cornelia, she says.

Yes.

The click of the door, Eva's practiced gait as she makes her way up Norris Crescent toward the streetcar stop. Andor watches, from his window, the form of Eva. In this suit and swing coat, with her pointy little boots and flecks of snow swatting at her legs, she is like the figures in his own paintings. An elegant triangle.

Here's another thing Andor has waited for: a response from William Ronald. Nearly a week he's waited. It comes in the early afternoon, twenty minutes or so before Cornelia finishes school. A hollow ring of the telephone.

Listen, says Bill. *Simpson's got the final say, and they wanted work that fit well with their new line.*

New line?

Line of furniture.

Ah.

We tried to put something together that matched the palette of the furniture. It wasn't personal, but everything of yours was pinks and blues and the upholstery, it was all oranges and greens and reds.

You could have told me the colors of . . . of the line. I work in reds and greens also.

It just didn't work out this time, says Bill, and the finality of the statement hangs and hangs.

Next time, says Bill.

What does Andor say, Bess? *Next time, don't bother.* He can't be sure whether he says this aloud or thinks it as he hangs up the phone. Lately, his mind has been doing this to him: playing tricks with his memory. Also, he's had little outbursts, mostly when alone. The tossing aside of a pencil, too violent, that leaves a grey mark on the wall where its soft lead breaks. Sometimes, a Hungarian swear that eats its way from his gut out into the world. If you were here now, in Andor's afternoon-dark living room, you might be able to give him some relief by telling him, no, your response was only in your mind. Or, perhaps, yes, you could say: you've done it. You have cut the final and only thread attaching you to the Toronto art scene. But don't worry—I've read it in books, when I was curious about you. You'll get your visa. You'll get to New York, a few miserable years from now. And you'll never return to Toronto. Maybe you'll never think on it again.

But you aren't there. Andor is alone. What to do, now? What to do? Sometimes, in moments like this, he makes furious art, but this time he can't face it. The very look of his drawing table is something menacing, a flat and dangerous animal. The colors of his paints, in their gnarled tubes, all wrong.

Sometimes, air. Air is correct, in this moment. Despite everything, despite the way the city makes his gut feel as if it is pierced and hung from a meat hook, he cannot deny the pleasant separateness of Norris Crescent, its hardscrabble children playing in the street, and its view of the gray lake, waves rising and falling. Sometimes, sailboats. Across the bay, the city skyline, its flat factory smoke and predictably triangular rooftops.

Andor walks as far as he can toward the lake, despite the weather. Seats himself on a bench that looks out on everything. Here are his little sketchbook and pencil, tucked, where they always live, in his coat pocket. He is drawing something. No, not drawing. Writing an essay.

"I live on Norris Crescent, Mimico."

Some music has started up: a wonderful jazz piano that drifts from the sky, it seems, down toward the lake. Who, on Norris Crescent, plays music like this? The last time Andor heard, and truly enjoyed, jazz—well, that was in another time, another place, gone now. But this, he enjoys. It seems to amble down to the foot of Norris Crescent with an easy gait, sit beside him on the bench, sling one ankle over a knee. It seems to say, go on, write, I'll just be here, feeling the absurdity of the world alongside you.

"It is well for an artist to live here, where I look on an expanse of sky, on trees, small cottages, and on the bay of Lake Ontario."

What more to say?

"I live with my wife, Eva, and our daughter, Cornelia, seven years old."

Cornelia. He has forgotten to pick up Cornelia.

Six—A Palace for Horses

When Mr. Franceschini returns to Martha Villa, weak and broken, bald from chemotherapy, pushed around in a wheelchair with a cashmere blanket thrown over his tired legs, he is met by a line of well-wishers. Groundskeepers who pull open the wrought iron gates, housekeepers and the maids and his brother Leonard and his own dear wife Annie and—there she is—Martha, princess Martha, so much older than she was when he left.

Try not to imagine yourself as Martha, Bess, though it is tempting—her beautiful life, her ponies, her ribbon bows and the vista she owns, straight across Humber Bay to the pier, the King Eddie hotel, the beach. Hard not to view the whole Franceschini-era property through Martha's young eyes.

Martha won't leave her dad's side, won't stop asking questions—*Was it terrible in the camp, Dad? What did you eat? Did you get mom's and my letters?*

Your dad's tired, says Annie. They're sitting in the greenhouse. She's loading up a plate for him. Deviled eggs. Little toasts with salmon and asparagus. *No more with the questions.*

Terrible, no. Humiliating—maybe. After all he'd done for this country, building roads, hotels, battleships, to be—the most sanitary of words—*interned*. All because of a horse. One beautiful horse.

But, it could have been worse. There were men of all sorts at Camp 33. Japanese, Germans, rich and poor. The Italians, though: these were the men he grew to know best. Others like him, who'd come to Canada with nothing. This he explains to Martha, later that day, as she wheels him around the garden, down by the lip of the lake.

I was fifteen when I came here, you understand? A boy.

Of course she understands. She's heard this story hundreds of times.

Now look what we have. He gestures around, generally, at the property and the lake and the city skyline, itself. Angry somehow, his gesture. Like he could swat the whole city away.

The lake, the beautiful lake. While her father was away, Martha visited it often—thinking of him, yes, but also of Duchess, off prancing somewhere in Italy. Duchess, with fiery flank and flared nostrils and gentle mien. She'd been Martha's horse, Martha had thought. She remembered standing on a stepladder in front of Duchess's stall, the horse's warm soft nose and sweet breath on her shoulder. You know this, Bess, because you know what little girls think of when they don't understand the adult world that surrounds them, when they have just begun to suspect the intentions of the grown-ups.

Perhaps, like you, they felt the push and pull of warring parents, of lawyers, of counselors, of the law. Perhaps, like Martha, their fathers were taken away by a number of official men, and in the waiting-time they forgot something about their fathers, like the smell of their hugs or the angle of their smiles. When such a thing happens, a little girl thinks of horses.

More than ever before, Mr. Franceschini is visited by people now. Lines of small business owners, hats crushed to their chests, snaking around the parlor and into his study. Politicians—local and, more and more often, provincial, national. Some sit on benches in the garden, where, in the fountain, four stone frogs spit onto an overjoyed putti. And Italian friends who stop Martha on her way out of the house or coming home from school—*I knew your daddy when we were just little boys*—always seem to be around.

Martha and her mother, sitting together in the living room. Mother is reading a book; Martha is doing homework. Laughter carries over from the study, where men in the construction business are gathered.

This house, says her mother, *is too small.*

Mr. Franceschini has an idea. He announces it at the dinner table.

A palace for horses.

Martha rolls the idea around in her mind for a moment. She imagines a king horse on his throne, a queen horse in a velvet robe. Princes and princesses—those would be the ponies.

Her mother has already leaned back in her chair, crossed her arms.

Now wait, wait, wait, wait, says Mr. Franceschini. He reaches back onto the buffet for a pile of renderings. Here are photos of a property looking out at the Laurentians, an artist's renderings of grand, gleaming stables, a mansion, a guest house, a smoking room, a games room, a greenhouse, an indoor pool, everything monogrammed, oxblood leather and glorious old carriages and antlers, so many antlers. He shows his wife a picture of a rose.

A secret garden, all for you.

He unrolls a blueprint. It unrolls and unrolls.

That place is a monstrosity, says Annie. *Who needs all that space?*

But you said that this house was too small, says Martha.

Her father smiles.

It's a waste of money, Jim, says Annie. *It's show-offy.*

So, what's wrong with showing off? Don't we deserve to show off? After all we've done?

Annie rearranges the napkin on her lap, purses her lips.

Mr. Franceschini, pointing out at the lake, the skyline. *I built that city.*

I know, Jim.

Anyways, he continues, *I already bought the property. Got a very good deal.*

A little zing of excitement in Martha. A palace for horses!

Can I have my own horse? she asks.

Sweetheart, you can have ten horses.

When will it be finished?

It isn't started yet. We've got to sell Martha Villa first.

That terrible dropping feeling.

I've got some guys interested in it. They're coming to see the property next week.

Already Annie is wiping her mouth with her napkin, getting up from the table. She leaves the room. With careful hands Mr. Franceschini smooths out the plans in front of him, as if they're ancient scrolls.

You're going to sell Martha Villa to some guys?

Somehow, now, the image of Duchess, a week after the Italian stranger came to Martha Villa, being reluctantly loaded into a horse trailer. Her eyes rolled wildly, then, looking back at Mr. Franceschini, who cooed at her to settle, settle, and at Martha, who swiped tears from her cheeks. She would never tell this to Dad—never—but, in the months, years he was interned, she thought just as much of Duchess as of him. Maybe more. Sometimes, in *LIFE* magazine, photographs of the war's devastation, bombed-out Italian villages that were nothing but skeletons of places, empty windows like sockets in a skull. She imagined Duchess stepping timidly through that rubble, her beautiful slender legs matted with brick dust and mud. Somewhere, a baby crying. Martha would often imagine this at night after she'd gone to bed, and tears would roll hotly into her ears and down her neck onto the pillow. Comforting, to feel something for someone she loved.

You used to do this at night, too, Bess. Maybe every girl cries at night just to feel tears crawling into the shells of her ears, thumping the pillow where they land. But you are not every girl; you are Martha, and Martha cried because she couldn't save what she'd lost, and because she knew that Duchess was gone, that her father was gone, even when he'd returned. She knew that her own home would be gone, and that all the grand estates of Mimico would one day tumble or decay or be knocked down, that this would be a neighborhood of struggling artists and motels and stumbling drunks and little fires on crags and then condos, glass and steel, slicing the sky, and the rich on white boats and commuters crushed together on the Long Branch streetcar, and that even she would die. Martha knew everything that would happen.

Two men arrive—brothers, maybe twins, in strangely matched suits. Longo and Longo. You'll recognize this name from the checks you sign each month—*Longo Brothers Properties*. The kind woman in the office who takes your checks lives in the penthouse at the top of your building, Oscar Peterson's old place. They say she's the mistress of a Longo. When you came home, once, to the scene of a domestic fight, the hallway on your floor streaked with blood and dotted with punches in the drywall, the Longos sent a repairman and bleach.

The Longos: some Italians Mr. Franceschini knows from somewhere—he seems to know every Italian in the city. Martha watches from her bedroom window as her dad, walking again, walks them around the property, opening outbuilding doors, pointing. The brothers, heads swiveling this way and that, taking it all in: the vast grounds, the stables, the ring, the garden, the greenhouse, and the lake. The lake seems to glisten today, showing off for these two. Saying, *aren't I pretty?*

The Longos think so. Already, they envision buildings. Tall apartment buildings dotting the site, the house itself divided into luxury apartments. Knock down this greenhouse and there can even be a building here next to the garden, giving it a Sicilian feel. They make large and excited arm gestures. Mr. Franceschini agrees—yes, this would make a very nice courtyard, indeed, for an apartment complex. Why don't we go inside and hammer out a deal?

Martha, in her bedroom. Can she leave the house named after her, the horse ring, the garden, the beautiful lake, the city skyline, her school, her friends? They have different schools in Quebec. Everyone speaks French.

Outside, the Longos are pointing. They point straight up. What's there? Nothing Martha can see. But, she hears. And what she hears—is it possible it comes from that empty spot in the sky that, now, all three men and several grooms stare at? This piano music, clear and confident, full of swagger and elegance, doing a muscular dance down and out, across the garden, the ring, the lake.

Martha is in the yard, now, standing with this ever-growing group of people who look up, up at sound and mystery. Here is Uncle Leonard, clenching a cigar between his teeth. Sometimes the lake can play tricks with sound, he says. Here is her mother, who puts two hands on Martha's shoulders as she stares. However much her mother resists it, one finger taps along with the music.

Seven—Oscar Peterson Plays "Round Midnight"

When he sits at the piano, Oscar Peterson's socks go on and on and on. He's a big man. He has to tuck himself into the instrument, legs bent at what looks like an uncomfortable angle. Trouser hem creeps up, revealing the trouser sock—brown, conservative, and seemingly endless, like the cosmos. This is what the piano tuner thinks, anyway.

If you were here beside the piano tuner, Bess, watching Oscar Peterson play, you might feel the music spooling through your own body: liquid and smooth. And you, too, might marvel at the socks, at the simplicity of them, a simplicity that says: these socks don't matter. The music matters.

The piano tuner, of course, waiting for Oscar Peterson's approval. Even after so many years of tending to this particular piano, he can make mistakes. Oscar Peterson will find them. He'll point them out—politely, of course—but the piano tuner knows to wait for the end of the music. The result is his own private concert. Only a sour note here or there. Just like life. The piano tuner sits on the couch.

What to do now, Bess? There's no more story to tell.

There's only the music, and the view from the penthouse as the sun sets: the sharp winking needle of the CN Tower, the old triangular roof of the Royal York Hotel, the dappled breasts of ducks and geese. And the lake, gilded orange, that carries away the cargo of the past and delivers new waves, new scents, new elsewheres to smooth the rocky shore.

ACKNOWLEDGMENTS

These stories first appeared in the following publications:

American Short Fiction: "Signs"
Ecotone: "A Beautiful Song, Very Melancholy and Very Old"
Indiana Review: "Bad"
The Gettysburg Review: "A General Confusion Overtook the Whole Vicinity"
Story online: "Machines of Another Era"
Alaska Quarterly Review: "Helena, Montana"
Barrelhouse online: "Make It as Beautiful as You Can"
Carousel: "Daguerreotypes"
Alice Blue: "Lord Byron's Teen Lover, Claire Clairmont"
Michigan Quarterly Review: "Talking Dolls"
SmokeLong Quarterly: "A Collector"
Covered with Fur: "Are You Running Away?"
Wigleaf: "How Do You Deal with the Horribly Cruel Things People Say to You Throughout Your Life?" and "A Bird of Uncertain Origin"
Berkeley Fiction Review: "Any Little Morsel"
Versal: "The Garnet Cave"
The Cincinnati Review: "The Stories You Write About Mimico"

Thank you:

To the editors who first gave these stories homes. I'm particularly grateful for the ongoing support and/or excellent editorial guidance of Scott Garson at *Wigleaf*, Anna Lena Phillips Bell and Beth Staples at *Ecotone*, Megan M. Garr, Anna Arov, and Robert Glick at *Versal*, as well as to Bill Henderson at Pushcart Press.

To the writers who've lent their support to this book: Amber Sparks, Anne Valente, Matt Bell, and my former teachers Josh Weil, Leah Stewart, Chris Bachelder, and Michael Griffith.

To Michael Czyzniejewski, the late Wendell Mayo, and Lawrence Coates at Bowling Green State University; the fiction faculty of University of Cincinnati; Mark Blagrave, Robert Lapp, and Heather Marcovitch at Mount Allison University; and Randall Kenan at the Sewanee Writers' Conference, for their mentorship. Special thanks and love to my first creative writing teacher and dear friend Jennifer Walcott.

To the Sewanee Writers' Conference for giving me the confidence to keep writing, and to the Corporation of Yaddo for the wonderous gift of time.

To my chair, Angela Vietto, and my colleagues in the English Department at Eastern Illinois University, for their continued support.

To my Bowling Green friends who read or heard some of these stories in their infancy, especially Jess Vozel and Brad Felver. And to Jen Fawkes and Sarah Strickley at University of Cincinnati, for their brilliant reading and writing.

To Kyle McCord for his faith in this project, his encouragement, and the skill and heart he puts into everything he does at Gold Wake. It's a privilege to have such a thoughtful poet as an editor. To Hannah Nuss for her support of the book. To Nick Courtright for designing a cover "that will shock the shit out of everyone," and to Barbara Bourgoyne for her careful work in setting the type.

To the people who understand me best, for believing that this book would actually be published one day: Tiffany Bayliss, Tim Jones, Megan Jones, Heidi Ebert, Alex Callahan, Amelia Haller,

Brad Modlin, Thalia Kapica, Victoria McCaffrey, Rochelle Hurt, Sherwin Tjia, Luke Geddes, Ian Golding, Andrea Valliere, Andrew Bales, and Pierre Malloy.

To my mom for her tall, tall bookcases and for being my first reader, first editor, and first champion, and to my dad for teaching me how to tell a good story. To my stepmom, for reading and appreciating and sewing.

To James the hound dog, who loves unabashedly and cuddles with all of his might, and to Woody Skinner the writer, who's the best, smartest, and funniest person in the world, as well as a brilliant editor, savvy publicist, and certified bacon chef. Thank you for your love.

ABOUT THE AUTHOR

Bess Winter's work has been awarded a Pushcart Prize and the American Short[er] Fiction Prize, and appears in *American Short Fiction, Gettysburg Review, Alaska Quarterly Review, Ecotone*, W.W. Norton's *Flash Fiction International*, and elsewhere. Originally from Toronto, Canada, she's an Assistant Professor of English at Eastern Illinois University. She lives in Urbana, IL.